THE WISH OF A THOUSAND CRANES

MIGUEL SANDOVAL RUIZ

Created with Vellum

CONTENTS

I

MIASMA

They were corpses. They were living corpses.

The feeling of inadequacy and self-loathing can make the silence loud. This can be especially discouraging, as it can have a profound impact on one's morale. Unfortunately, Borden was all too familiar with this experience, feeling lost, stuck, and frustrated with himself.

Despite his passion for the arts, Borden found himself unemployed and lacking direction. He turned to writing as a means of channeling his energy, hoping it would provide a sense of purpose. However, he quickly discovered that the blank page was far more intimidating than he had expected.

Sitting in front of his computer, Borden was paralyzed by indecision. He stared at his claw-like hands, hoping they would somehow produce a story with the click of the keyboard. But the words wouldn't come. His mind was a mess of ideas and possibilities, none of which seemed good enough to pursue.

Borden felt as though the silence was taunting him. The lack of sound was a constant reminder of his own inadequacies.

Borden's previous job as a remote sales associate was a monotonous and unfulfilling experience. Borden had always dreamed of having a career in the creative field, where he could use his natural talents and love of entertainment to create something that truly resonated with people. It was only when he was unexpectedly laid off that he realized that losing his job was a blessing in disguise.

THERE WAS a time when the sound of Borden's fingers tapping on the keyboard brought him joy and excitement, similar to a child's delight in hearing Christmas carols. He found inspiration in the clicking of the keys as each word flowed effortlessly. However, as time passed, that once delightful sound became unpleasant, losing its charm.

With every press of the backspace key, Borden's enthusiasm dwindled. Doubt crept in, and he began to question his abilities as a writer. What did he really know about writing, anyway?

As he struggled to find his footing, Borden realized that writing was not as simple as he had initially thought. It required discipline, patience, and a willingness to face the many challenges that came with the creative process. There were days when the words flowed effortlessly, and others when he found himself staring at a blank screen, struggling to put a single sentence together.

All roads lead to death. That is inevitable.

[BACKSPACE]

We choose our paths, but it is impossible to venture into uncharted waters without a map of where we have been. All choices will be a coin flip.

[BACKSPACE]

We simplify life to be a road that leads to death. It might help decide what the important things in life are.

[BACKSPACE]

Borden disliked pretentiousness but acknowledged the value of expressing emotions. He believed readers should look beyond pretentiousness to uncover the valuable message within. Of course, sometimes something is just that, pretentious.

Being unemployed felt like writing his novel. Rather, his hands being stagnant on the keys, it was his body that felt stuck. Stuck to that chair. To that floor. In that house. On that ground, that would one day swallow him.

Borden wondered if there was more to his condition than writer's block or stress. Over the past few days or weeks, he can't pinpoint it precisely, he has been getting headaches that made him feel disconnected from reality, and something, physical or psychological, was causing them. He was experiencing an odd phase.

Odd might be the wrong word here. A door he left open was then closed. That's odd. A logical explanation for that is possible, but albeit—odd.

Hearing a voice that says you don't belong requires a

different type of adjective to describe it.

BORDEN SETTLED into his swivel chair, leaning back and forth as he contemplated. His expression reflects that of Auguste Dobin's statue, with his chin nestled in his hand as he searched for inspiration. He stared at the screen in front of him; the cursor taunting him with its ceaseless blink.

Indulging in the habitual act of procrastination, Borden's eyes wandered over to the framed picture on the wall, using the guise of being lost in thought. As long as he was contemplating his writing, he felt justified in allowing his mind to wander.

As he stared at the image, he wondered about the concept of time. About how photographs capture moments frozen at a specific point in time, while life continues to move forward. The photo reminded him of the fleeting nature of life, and how it was important to cherish every moment.

The philosophical connection between the photograph and his writing became clear. Just as a photograph captured a moment in time, his writing captured his thoughts and emotions in a particular moment, allowing him to relive and reflect on them in the future.

"Hi."

"Olivia?" He asked, shifting his eyes away from the computer screen.

No one.

He turned his attention away from the door.

"TURN ON THE LIGHT, dear. It's not good for your eyes," Olivia said as she flips the switch.

Borden jumped out of his skin.

Olivia wore a proud grin on her face as Borden remarked, "You almost gave me a heart attack."

He turned his head to look at Olivia, who was watching him with a mixture of concern and amusement.

"Open a window too. It's stuffy in here," she said, leaning down for a kiss.

Borden smiled and watched her leave as she exited the room.

She always seems to know how to exit a room.

As Olivia left the room, Borden's smile faded away. The thought of being watched remained like a dark cloud hovering over him.

Borden fixated his eyes back on the photo, tracing the lines of their smiling faces with a hint of nostalgia.

I can't believe how much time has passed since that day.

He remembered the excitement and anticipation as they said their vows, promising to love and support each other.

But it seems like he's been failing to uphold his end of the bargain. The job loss hit him hard, and it's been a struggle to regain his footing. He knew Olivia had noticed his lack of motivation and drive, and it was not fair to her. She deserved better than a husband who was stuck in a rut. With a determined look on his face, Borden resolved to make a change and become the partner that Olivia deserved.

I can write about that. Love.

The idea of dedicating a novel to his wife filled him with inspiration. He felt a surge of excitement as he thought about the possibility of creating something special for her.

The more he thought about it, the more he realized it could be the perfect anniversary present. He had never been the best at gift-giving, but this idea felt like the right fit. He knew the journey wouldn't be easy, but with Olivia by his side, he was ready to take on anything.

I can write about love and printers, and other computer accessories.

Borden chuckled to himself, feeling a sense of amusement at the thought of combining the themes of love and printers in his writing.

Despite the perceived insignificance of this knowledge, it had been a part of his life for so long that it had become a part of him. He recognized that sometimes the most unexpected sources of expertise can inspire the most creative works.

He swiveled his chair to type.

Hi Borden.

Borden leaned forward, squinting at the screen.

"What the hell," he said.

Borden pressed the backspace key, but it didn't seem to work. He tried pressing it multiple times.

Nothing worked. The computer had taken a mind of its own.

It typed:

Hi Borden. Hi Borden. Hi Borden. Hi Borden...

Borden's eyes scanned the words that filled the page, the computer possessed by an unknown force. He searched for a solution, trying to determine the cause of the sudden malfunction.

He pressed down on the power button to force a shut-down. No luck. Borden snapped the laptop shut.

That's great. Just when I had an idea.

Borden's head shot up at the sound of a loud thud outside. His eyes flickered to the open door. He froze, listening for any further sounds.

"Olivia? Everything okay?"

After a moment of silence, the creak of his chair echoed in the room as he stood up. His lanky frame rose, relieving the chair of the hours of his laborious writing.

Entering the kitchen, expecting to see Olivia, he found a note on the counter that read:

Long shift at the hospital. See you in the morning. Love ya.

Another long shift at the hospital, he thought to himself. What's new about that?

Borden felt a twinge of guilt and longing as he thought about his wife's long work hours. While he felt bitter about her absence, he understood her job demanded such commitment. He missed spending time with her, like watching movies together or strolling in the park. His frustration about his lack of work leads him to project his emotions onto her.

As the sole provider for their small family, consisting only of the two of them, he sometimes felt useless. His gaze shifted toward the refrigerator, and he noticed a calendar hanging by two magnets, showing that something special was on the horizon.

Oh, is that soon?

Borden's face lit up as he noticed a red "x" marked

below the date four days from the present, showing a special event. However, his excitement faded as he felt guilty about not being productive enough to earn a vacation.

Knock!

A knock at the door broke his concentration.

The sound was sharp and decisive, like the knock of someone who knew what they wanted. It reverberated through the room, causing a momentary pause in Borden's thoughts.

"Olivia," he said.

She must've forgot something.

"I'm coming."

The solitary knock on the door soon transformed into a ceaseless barrage of pounding.

"Okay, calm down. Damn, you're gonna break the door down."

The knocking began rattling his skull as if it were coming from inside of his head. His hands were figuratively prying his skull open to release the pain. As if a screwdriver was penetrating his occipital bone. The pounding intensified. The knocking culminated into one giant thump.

There it is again, that fucking sound.

Much louder than before, to be exact.

It stopped.

THE HANDS BURIED in his hair emerged, and Borden opened his eyes to find himself in an unfamiliar place. It was so dark around him, and a thick stillness filled the air. The sense of unease was overtaking him. He stood up, trying to keep his balance as his head spun. His eyes searched for any light source to orient himself with, but everything was so dark. So desolate.

Borden lifted his gaze towards the direction where the sky should be. Glints of light appeared, revealing the moon. It was a timid presence, but enough to offer Borden some visual cues about his surroundings. Aside from the fact he was outside, he was clueless about his location.

The soft glow of the moon drew Borden's eyes to the top of the hill. The cold, eerie winds carried the dense fog over the fields below. As he strained to listen, faint whispers reached his ears, confirming that he was not alone in this mysterious place.

The voices became clearer, though still muffled by the wind and distance. They sounded like hushed whispers, the conversations that people have when they don't want to be overheard. He couldn't make out any words, but the tones were urgent, and there was a sense of tension in the air.

As he walked, the ground beneath him felt uneven, causing him to stumble. It was moist and clumpy. But he kept being drawn to the light at the top of the hill like a moth to a flame.

Borden questioned the reality of his surroundings. He felt as if someone had trapped him in a dream, a nightmare that he couldn't escape from. In a moment of desperation, he pinched himself, hoping that it would wake him up from this surreal experience. But the sharp pain he felt only confirmed that he was not dreaming, at least not in the traditional sense.

Well, that's a load of bull.

The cold air nipped at his neck. Borden rubbed his hands together to generate some warmth as he made his way up the steep hill. His eyes darted around, wary of any sudden dips or holes in the ground. As he ascended, he noticed an odd sight below. The littered ground flourished with an array of trinkets and belongings as if their owners had discarded them. Watches, necklaces, shoes, and other personal effects one would think twice before leaving behind. Among the heap of items, Borden's eyes fixated on a small figurine of a crane.

Interesting.

He hesitated to touch the figurine, unsure of the reason for its abandonment. He decided it was better not to disturb anything.

The hill loomed before him, rising into the night. As he climbed, the trees on either side took on an unnatural appearance, their gnarled branches reached out like skeletal fingers in the darkness. Each step seemed to reveal more of them, contorted as if writhing in pain or torment. The rustling of leaves in the wind sounded like whispers, and the shadows they cast danced like specters. Borden shuddered, feeling as if he were trespassing in a realm where he didn't belong.

A myriad of voices chattered as he walked past.

"Why is he here?"

"Who is that?"

"He shouldn't be here. He's not ready," the voices said.

"Hello, is anyone there?" Borden asked.

He preferred not to have anyone answer him since he didn't see anyone around.

A swarm of crows descended upon him, their piercing caws filling the air as Borden reached the top. The birds were so many that they seemed to blot out the sky, and Borden could feel the wind from their wings as they flapped. They then moved in unison to a nearby patch of land, leaving Borden to wonder what had caused such a chaotic reaction.

Borden turned around, filled with regret for coming to this vantage point. However, as he looked back, it appeared everything that existed behind him was being erased with each step he took forward. He realized that there was no turning back now.

HE GLANCED BACK, watching as the area he had already passed through disappear from existence, like a collapsing bridge. Despite his unease, Borden continued forward, drawn by an inexplicable force towards the murder of crows.

No way back, Borden. There's nothing back there, he reminded himself.

The sky captured his attention. Something remarkable, it seemed.

Is that?

He came to an abrupt stop, struck with awe by the breathtaking sight before him. The sky above seemed to have exploded into an array of colors, resembling the Northern Lights, but ten times more magnificent. The colors danced and swirled, creating a hypnotizing display that left Borden spellbound. He stood there for what felt like hours, immersed in the moment's beauty.

THE SOLAR SYSTEM? That's Jupiter! That's Saturn!

BORDEN FELT a sense of peace wash over him. The fear and confusion that had plagued him dissipated, replaced by a sense of wonder and amazement.

This is incredible.

Borden's expression was short-lived. Quickly it turned from awe to dread as he realized what he'd been looking at in the sky. It was the planet Earth, looming above him like a harbinger of doom.

That's Earth? No, it can't be. I'm on Earth, aren't I?

He couldn't believe his eyes.

BORDEN TRIED to convince himself that this was just a dream, that the surreal scene before him was not real. He pinched himself again, hoping to wake up from this nightmare, but the view of the planet Earth floating in the sky remained. He closed his eyes and took a deep breath, trying to calm himself down. When he opened his eyes again, the planet was still there, taunting him with its impossible existence.

The brightness of the celestial body overhead revealed the entire field before him, but instead of feeling comforted by the illumination, Borden wished he could have turned the lights off again.

Branches, vines, and wind joined the choir of voices ahead as he walked further. The same voices he had heard earlier on the breeze. His spirit sank as he saw the source of the voices.

Borden tried to gather his courage.

It's only a dream.

It's only a dream.

What are they doing? They're just standing there.

THESE PEOPLE WERE LIKE STATUES. As he approached, the sea of motionless bodies became more apparent. The murder of crows perched on some and cawed at others. He couldn't discern any distinct features, and the closer he got, the more his body tensed up. The wind carried a putrid odor, so foul that it made Borden gag.

What is that smell? He thought to himself. Pinching his shirt over his nose. *Smells like formaldehyde.*

He realized. They were corpses. They were living corpses. A graveyard seemed like the perfect place for the land of the dying, and Borden's suspicions were confirmed as he spotted small blocks of cement scattered about.

Tombstones?

He pressed on.

The sounds of moans and groans became a constant backdrop to this eerie place, with the cawing of a crow adding to the unsettling atmosphere. It was far from a symphony; more like a chaotic cacophony.

"Hello!" he called out, both hands on the side of his mouth.

Suddenly, they began rotating, like a synchronized dance. And then, as if on cue, they all turned to face him, their eyes stared at him with an empty, lifeless gaze.

And then the sound began. It was a low, sonorous moan that seemed to emanate from the very depths of the earth. It was a sound that could suck the essence out of any living thing, and Borden could feel it vibrating in his bones. The howl of a banshee's cry pierced the midnight air, adding the cherry on top to this insidious nightmare.

A crow appeared, flapping its wings in front of Borden's face, causing him to flinch and swing his arms to shoo it away. The bird dodged his hands and landed on the ground beside him. Irritated by the crow's presence, Borden glared at it, clenching his fist in frustration.

As he looked closer, he noticed the crow had perched itself on top of a tombstone.

ANGIER BORDEN

1982-2023

Borden ran his fingers over the carved letters of the tombstone, trying to comprehend how it was possible. The crow's unwavering stare fixed on him, almost as if it were trying to guide him. As he read the name, a sense of terror gripped him. The name on the tombstone was his own, along with the year 2023, which was the current year.

Borden stood up, only to vomit over his own grave. The stench grew stronger. As he tried to cough out the last bits of bile from his mouth, he realized the bodies have surrounded him.

The corpses, with their snarls and probing eyes, stood face-to-face with him. Their hands reached out, and Borden screamed as they overwhelmed him, pushing him down into the grave. The crow watched from its perch; menacing, blood-stained eyes fixed on Borden. It seemed as if the crow was the ringleader of this macabre circus.

One of the corpses said, "You don't belong here. It's too late for us. You need to go back."

As they lowered Borden further into the grave, darkness enveloped him, and the weight of the dirt above pressed down on his chest, making it hard for him to breathe. He realized with horror that he was being buried alive.

Wake up, Borden! Wake up!

He continued to sink lower and lower, his cries silenced by the suffocating earth. At last, he reached the bottom, crashing onto the solid ground below, gasping for air.

He could breathe again.

What the fuck?

. . .

He looked up to see a hole in his kitchen ceiling, which was closing itself shut. Dirt continued to trickle down onto his face as it sealed itself shut.

Borden lay sprawled out on his kitchen floor, gasping for air and coping to understand what had just transpired. He felt immobilized, drained, and helpless, as though someone had glued him to the frigid tiles he had installed years ago. He couldn't recall them ever feeling so cold. Every breath he took produced a visible puff of smoke, a testament to the chilling temperature he was experiencing.

My soul is seeping out of me, he imagined. *How poetic.*

It would be even more poetic for Olivia to find him lying there.

What could she imagine?

Borden's legs were wobbling as he struggled to stand, feeling as if they could give way at any moment. The room was spinning, and he had to brace himself against the countertop to avoid falling over. His vision was blurry, but he could make out the faint outline of his couch across the room. The sound of his labored breathing filled his ears, and his head was throbbing with pain.

He made it to the couch, sinking into the soft cushions that seemed to embrace his tired body. He could feel the warmth radiating from the fabric as it enveloped him, and he closed his eyes, taking a moment to catch his breath and regain his composure.

This is much better. His eyes closed. *I hope Olivia is okay.*

2

THE FOREIGN SILHOUETTE

She stood over Borden, the moonlight piercing through the window, casting her shadow on the wall. The painted silhouette of her body.

Dr. Borden stumbled out of the hospital doors, her face contorted in anguish. Dr. Borden's face showed the weight of the day's events, etched deep into her furrowed brow and down-turned eyes. No matter how hard she tried, her quivering hands betrayed her true feelings. Her white lab coat, once pristine, now clung to her like a burden.

Her eyes scanned the busy street, her attention momentarily drawn to the flashing lights of an ambulance parked nearby. Her badge caught the light, reflecting the image of a proud and smiling Olivia, a stark contrast to the defeated woman wearing it now.

For a moment, she simply stood there, taking in the sounds of the surrounding city - the honking of horns, the hum of the streetlights. Her thoughts drifted to the patient she had just saved, the close call that had shaken her to her core. A tiny achievement in an unwavering battle.

Despite her years of experience in healthcare, Dr. Borden knew she would never become desensitized to the feeling of helplessness that came when it seemed like a patient was close to death.

Olivia was feeling overwhelmed and exhausted. She'd been working tirelessly, juggling multiple patients, and leading the new residents during their rounds. To make matters worse, she couldn't stop worrying about her husband, Borden.

They've been together for a decade, with six of those years as a married couple. Olivia has always been the primary earner, but it's never been an issue for either her or Borden. They've always made it work, their partnership functioning seamlessly to create a life that they both deserve.

This week had been especially hard on her, and she was struggling to keep it together.

As a child, Olivia spent many afternoons at the hospital, wandering the halls and spending time with patients while her mother worked there. These experiences may have nurtured her and guided her toward a healthcare career.

However, the time has passed, and the same halls that she once explored as a curious spectator are now the same halls that she navigates as a facilitator, leading her team through the challenges of the healthcare industry.

. . .

Time is a finite resource that inexorably ends, whether we hoard it or give it away freely. Time is impartial and unrelenting. For Borden, time is a cruel reminder of his shortcomings and a measure of his love for Olivia. As for Olivia, time holds the power of life and death over her patients.

Olivia took a moment to compose herself, wiping away the tears that had gathered at the corners of her eyes. She took a deep breath and straightened up her scrubs, steeling herself for whatever the rest of the day may hold.

There was something bittersweet about close calls, like the one she just had. While they are undoubtedly traumatizing, they also serve as a reminder of what could have happened and a validation of the hard work she and her team have put in to prevent the worst-case scenario.

Borden's greatest concern for Olivia was the toll her work takes on her heart. He worried that her empathetic nature and dedication to building connections with her patients would eventually kill her. Olivia is not one of those doctors who saw healthcare purely as a business.

Every patient who walked through the doors of the hospital had a place in her heart, and her mind was constantly active with thoughts of them. Even during a quiet dinner at home, something might preoccupy her with a patient's condition or diagnosis. She'll zone out and wonder how Ms. Daisy is doing.

He feared that the stress of her responsibilities could one day cause something as serious as an aneurysm. Though it may be morbid to think about, Borden was only concerned for his wife's well-being.

Even when it came down to fictional characters, Olivia

couldn't help but empathize with their pain and struggle. It's just who she was. However, when duty calls, she knew how to silence those voices and focus on the task at hand. She could switch from the emotional Olivia to the determined and attentive doctor in a matter of seconds.

As Olivia made her way down the hallway, a sharp voice cut through her thoughts. It's the receptionist, calling her attention to hand her an urgent message. Olivia's years of experience in healthcare were clear in her quick response, immediately shifting gears to attend to any pressing issue.

Call me back. It's about "you know who," I'd also like to know if you're coming over tonight. I'll be making my famous casserole. Love you.

I hope everything's okay, she thought, reading her mother's note.

"Thanks, Sarah,"

"No problem, Dr. Borden."

"How are things going today out here? Slow?" Olivia asked.

"Nothing out of the ordinary," she replied.

"I might have a chance to call now then."

"I'll page you if anything."

Olivia nodded and headed toward the pediatrics department.

Despite its modest size, the hospital provided several essential amenities, including WiFi, vending machines, coffee stations, workstations with computers, storage rooms, waiting rooms, an information desk, and much more. There was a locker room for the workers and a small break room that sees little use lately because of the staff's recent layoffs. The cafeteria, however, was a different story.

It was boastful in size, capable of catering to the volumes of people that inhabit it, and staffed by a team of five workers, most of whom have been there since Olivia's mother retired. The cafeteria held a special place in Olivia's heart, as she spent most of her childhood there.

Everyone knew each other, and very well. They maintained a professional rapport and treated each other with an undeniable level of respect.

Olivia settled down in the empty pediatrics waiting room, taking a seat by the small table where children usually play. A bead toy on wires caught her attention, reminding her of how easily entertained children can be. The room was unusually quiet, giving her some privacy to make a phone call.

Not long after Olivia dialed the number, Mariana answered the phone with a hint of concern in her voice. The two exchanged formalities before Mariana got to the point.

"How is everything, Oli?"

Olivia hesitated before sharing too much detail about her work situation with her mother, as she knew how much it could affect her. She didn't want to add to Mariana's worries unnecessarily. Olivia remembered the last time she had shared about a patient's death during surgery. Mariana was deeply affected and had trouble sleeping for a few weeks. The apple didn't fall far from the tree.

"It's okay, ma, you know how it is," Olivia said.

Olivia knew that even though she had reassured her mother, Mariana would still worry. Olivia accepted that this is just how her mother was wired. She has an innate ability to sense when something was off with her child. It was like a modern-day superpower.

"How's Angi?" Mariana asked.

Mariana knew it was a sensitive topic but felt it was important to ask about.

Olivia responded with a fragile sense of conviction, "Borden is good, ya know."

"I trust you. You know what's best for you," she said, her voice filling with warmth and love. "Just remember that I'll always be here for you, no matter what. You can talk to me about anything, okay?"

Olivia felt a wave of comfort wash over her. Even though she didn't like to burden her mother with her work, it was nice to know that she had someone to turn to if she needed to.

"Thank you, Mom. I appreciate that, and yes. I think I will be coming over tonight," she said, feeling grateful for her mother's unwavering support.

They exchanged a few more pleasantries before ending the call. Olivia took a deep breath and headed back to work, feeling a renewed sense of purpose and determination.

OLIVIA REMINISCED about her childhood spent waiting for her mother's shifts to end. It wasn't always easy, and sometimes she felt annoyed or bored. But looking back now, she realized how much those moments have shaped her. It was during those times that she developed her love for anatomy, flipping through coloring books and learning about the human body.

And it was during those times that she developed her empathy for others, watching as her mother cared for patients and formed bonds with them. She felt grateful for those experiences now, even though they weren't always easy.

"ARE YOU DONE YET, MA?" A Young Olivia asked.

She replayed a memory in her head.

"Soon sweetie, soon."

"Okay, I'm hungry!"

"Here's a dollar. Go to the vending machine!"

I MUST'VE BEEN SUCH a handful.

Olivia was grateful for her mother's sacrifices and always tried to make the most of the time they had together. Mariana instilled values in her daughter that would help her navigate the world. She taught her the importance of empathy, hard work, and dedication. Olivia internalized these lessons and made them her own, using them as the foundation of her medical career.

Olivia kept thinking about the moments when her mother would come to check on her during those long waiting periods. Mariana would always come with a smile, bringing snacks or books to keep her entertained.

"IT'S TIME TO GO, SWEETIE," Mariana said.

"Finally! What took you so long?"

She was working hard! *To keep food on the table and a roof over our heads,* Olivia thought, watching this memory play out in front of her.

I'll call her back later and ask how she's doing. I forgot to ask how she was doing.

The hospital intercom paged Doctor Borden, seeking her immediate help. She left, leaving behind her inner child in the waiting room to play. There was no time for reminiscing right now.

Olivia joined the residents in Patient Room C, one of the critical care units. The patient's heart rate had skyrocketed, and everyone was on high alert. Despite the urgency of the situation, Olivia saw this as an opportunity for the residents to learn. She took a moment to gather her thoughts before taking action.

"We have to slow the heart rate!"

"Good. What do we need?" Olivia asked the group with a sense of urgency, fully aware of the severity of the situation.

"Ventricular Fibrillation?" called out the other resident.

"Possibly. However, we must reduce the heart rate." Olivia said, waiting for an answer.

But time is of the essence. Finally, she answered it herself.

"We can practice vagal nerve maneuvers or administer an antiarrhythmic drug either orally or intravenously."

The residents nod and quickly take their positions, ready to assist in any way they can. Olivia knew that teamwork was crucial like these, and she valued the input of her colleagues. As they worked together to stabilize the patient, Olivia listened to their observations and answered their questions, weighing each suggestion before deciding. She knew that every second counted in critical care, but she also understood the importance of thoroughness and collaboration in providing the best possible outcome for the patient.

One resident rushed to administer the IV treatment, while others recorded notes and prepared the patient for the procedure. Olivia observed them with a sense of relief, appearing calm and collected. She wanted to instill confidence in her team, but inside, she felt fear creeping in. She was afraid that her decisions could lead to a worst-case scenario, afraid that her patient may not survive.

THE FIRST TIME Olivia lost a patient, it was a devastating experience that left her feeling helpless and hopeless. She struggled with self-doubt and guilt, wondering if she could have done anything differently to save the patient. Borden was there to comfort and reassure her, reminding her that medicine is not always predictable and that sometimes, despite their best efforts, patients can still pass away. Olivia had a hard time coping with the loss, often losing sleep and reviewing medical records, trying to do better next time. She even developed anxiety whenever she had to enter the room where it happened.

However, a few weeks later from the incident, she received a heartfelt letter from the family of the patient. They expressed gratitude for Olivia's efforts and praised her for never giving up on their loved one. The letter was a much-needed reminder for Olivia that despite the loss; she had made a positive impact on the patient and their family.

Soon after, a severely injured patient came in late one

evening. Despite being about to clock out for the night, Olivia jumped into action upon seeing the scene.

She worked tirelessly for hours, finally walking out of those doors with a sense of accomplishment. She wiped frustration from her brow and smiled at the family, who were eager to hear the verdict. This experience was a turning point for Olivia, a sign of hope in herself.

After they handled the situation in Patient Room C, Olivia made her final rounds and headed to her locker to get cleaned up. Inside, she had a picture of Borden with a cheeky expression, along with a Polaroid of an inside joke they shared. There were also pictures of cute puppies, reminiscent of a junior high school student decorating their first locker to express themselves.

She ran her fingers over the smooth surface of the picture of Borden, the inside joke written in bold letters making her smile. She took one last look around before closing her locker and headed towards the exit, the weight of her bag slung over her shoulder.

She looked at her watch, tracing the watch's face with her opposite hand. This watch was a gift from her husband, Borden.

Oh Borden, see you soon.

Eighteen grueling hours had come to a close. Olivia took a deep breath, savoring the feeling of finally being able to relax. Her feet were aching, and her eyes felt heavy, but she was grateful for the chance to go home.

This was just another day in the life of a doctor, she reminded herself. She recalled her longest shift ever, 58 hours after an accident involving over 50 people. To survive, she relied on endless cups of tea and a variety of quick snacks.

When she finally returned home, exhausted, Borden made sure she got the rest she needed. He even slept in the office to ensure his snoring wouldn't disturb her. Borden thoughtfully provided her with a little bell to ring in case she needed anything. It started as a joke, but weeks later, Olivia still rang the bell to call him over.

OLIVIA ARRIVED HOME, taken aback to find her husband completely passed out on the couch, and a mess–no, not just a mess–it was more like a landslide of dirt that had spilled onto her kitchen tiled floor.

"Borden!" Olivia shouted. "Borden, where did this come from?"

Borden lay curled up on the couch, his body slowly uncurling as Olivia approached him. He looked defeated, glancing at her and then at the floor, before casting one last glance at the ceiling.

"I fell through it," he said as he pointed and mimicked the trajectory of the fall. "I don't know what happened, but I'm glad you're home."

Olivia was too stunned to speak.

His voice faded out, relieved that she was finally home. He collapsed into unconsciousness.

Olivia stood with a puzzled expression on her face, her eyes fixed on the spot on the ceiling where Borden had pointed.

"He fell through that?" she said to herself, trying to make sense of his words.

She cast a glance around the room, searching for any sign of what he was referring to. Olivia's curiosity intensified as she searched for very specific clues, almost like a detective on a mission. It was not the reaction Borden would expect from her, especially if he were awake. She looked around the kitchen, then the living room, and finally, his office, her head moving quickly and decisively as if she were a burglar searching for hidden cameras.

"Just what do you think you're up to? This is not going to end well," she said.

She looked over at the calendar and said, "Just a little while longer."

Olivia assumed cleaning up the mess, her footsteps and grunts filling the room. Suddenly, Borden gasped for air as the sound of munching startled him. It was an image straight from a nature documentary. He opened his eyes like a butterfly emerging from its cocoon, only to witness an oddity that could only exist in a paranormal reality. Olivia was eating the dirt.

Olivia, what are you doing? He thought.

Half asleep, he questioned whether he was awake or dreaming. He got out a few words before conceding to sleep. "Why are you, Olivia? Why are you eating?–"

"I'll see you in the morning, Borden," she said ominously.

Olivia vanished into the dark hallway that led to their bedroom. An indistinguishable chanting broke the silence that followed. It sounded like an incantation, and the voice was not Olivia's. Such decibels were beyond her range. It appeared something else was being channeled through her.

The words came to a halt.

The door opened.

Olivia stepped out, footsteps that belonged to someone

much heavier than she was. She stood over Borden, the moonlight piercing through the window, casting her shadow on the wall.

The painted silhouette of her body.

EXCEPT IT WASN'T her body.

3

BORDEN THE BURDEN

Perhaps he has already lost her without realizing it.

The aroma of decay and the warmth of the sun streaming through the window stirred Borden awake. His nostrils quivered, as though recognizing the scent.

What's that smell?

He lifted his arm and gave a big whiff.

It's not me. Where did I smell this before?

"The graveyard!" He called.

Borden sprung off the couch and rushed over to the kitchen. To his surprise, someone had cleared the dirt.

Olivia, damnit. She didn't have to do that.

Borden felt guilty that Olivia had to come home and clean up after him after a long day at work. Although he didn't know where the dirt came from, he still felt responsible for the mess. It was as if he blinked and found himself surrounded by the dead. He couldn't shake off the feeling that something else came back with him, a souvenir from his nightmare. But it was just a dream, right?

As he contemplated which dream to share first with Olivia, Borden couldn't help but chuckle at the absurdity of the situation.

She was eating dirt!

The sight was grotesque, her hands clawing at the dirt and shoveling it into her mouth. Hunched over like a twisted gargoyle, it was an unsettling image.

He wondered if it was all just a bizarre dream. But the memory of the smell of rot and the sight of the corpses still drifted in his mind. He decided he would share the dream about the graveyard first, and save the kitchen mess for later. Maybe it would make for a funny story over breakfast.

"Olivia!"

No answer.

"Olivia! You home?"

He called out to her once more, but no response.

Is she not here again? I don't understand. She's always gone when I'm up.

"I guess she didn't have any breakfast today," Borden said, looking into the empty sink. "No cereal bowl."

He grabbed a cereal bowl for himself and opened the pantry, eagerly searching for his favorite cereal. Disappointingly, he couldn't seem to find it. Instead, he spotted his least favorite cereal, which ironically seemed to be stocked up.

"Why do we have this? We know we don't eat this garbage," he grumbled to himself, feeling slightly annoyed.

A small smirk formed on his face as he thought about Olivia eating dirt.

Maybe she skipped breakfast cause she had enough dirt!

WITH NO OTHER OPTION, he sits alone in the kitchen, chewing his not-so-favorite cereal. He stared at the ceiling in between bites, lost in thought about the strange dream he had.

The solar system had looked so cool, but the zombie things were terrifyingly real. Maybe he had sleepwalked and done some gardening in the kitchen.

He laughed, spilling some milk and cereal onto the table. "Yup, that's probably what happened," he said to himself.

But as he wiped up the mess, he got a nagging feeling that something was not right. The dream felt too real, too vivid. He tried to recall what the ghoulish fiends were saying to him as they pushed him down. They were speaking to him, saying he didn't belong there.

An idea sparked within him. He reached for a brand new spiral notebook from a drawer and jotted down his dream, hoping that writing it down would help him make sense of it all.

How convenient, he thought.

Journaling was never Borden's thing, but under these strange circumstances, it might be helpful to keep a log. He was the type to buy a planner every year and stop writing in it by February, only to buy a new one in July and repeat the cycle.

He wrote in his journal:

"Yesterday, or what feels like yesterday, my computer was

acting up. The words 'Hi Borden' kept being typed repeatedly. Soon after, I heard a loud noise from the kitchen. I assumed it was Olivia, but she had already left for work. When I went to check, my migraine hit me hard, and I can't remember anything else.

As for the "dream," I'm not sure when I fell asleep or passed out. Perhaps the pain from the migraine was too much. But in the dream, it was unsettling. I found myself in a field, no, a cemetery - a frigid and terror-inducing graveyard."

Borden tried to rationalize what had happened but failed continuously to explain the dream. The messengers in his dream. The corpses. Seeing his own tombstone and what it could signify.

He continued in his journal:

"I know dreams can be just that—just dreams. But this felt different. It felt like it meant something. It felt like a message. But what is the message? And who is sending it? And how is it all connected? I have so many questions and no answers. I just hope that writing it all down will help me make sense of it all."

He put down the pen.

The events from the previous night distracted Borden and the questions they brought forth. He didn't dwell on the bizarre image of his wife eating dirt; it seemed too surreal to be real.

He regretted having had little time to spend with her. Normally, this would bother him, since he cherishes the little time they have to interact before she goes off to work, but right now, he didn't seem to mind, as he was engrossed in trying to make sense of everything that was happening.

As he rinsed his cereal bowl, Borden's eyes darted toward the calendar hanging on the kitchen wall. Something didn't feel right.

"That's odd," he said to himself. "It's Wednesday, but it feels like Monday."

He wondered if he'd been living in a dream or if the dreams were affecting his real life. The constant headaches and momentary blackouts weren't helpful, either. The line between reality and dreams seemed to get blurrier by the day. It was becoming more difficult to distinguish between what was real and what wasn't.

Today will be different. He felt invigorated and focused after writing in his journal. As he prepared a cup of chamomile tea, the soothing aroma filled his senses, calming any remaining tension he may still have. He felt ready to tackle writing his novel, excited to dive into his creative world and leave the troubles of reality behind, at least for a little while.

Let's work on that novel, shall we?

On his way to the office, something about the mirror in the hallway captured his attention.

Upon reaching the mirror, he noticed that his reflection didn't quite match his movements. It's as if his reflection was moving a split second slower than he was. He blinked a few times, thinking it must be a trick of the light. Some strange delay.

But when he reached out to touch the glass, his hand passed through it as if the mirror were made of water. He jumped back, startled, and stared at the mirror in disbelief. His heart was racing, but it also filled him with an inexplicable curiosity. He took a deep breath and reached out his hand again, watching as nothing abnormal happened. It was solid.

I'm losing it, he thought.

He took another deep breath and stepped forward to face the mirror once more. This time, his reflection was back to normal. He chuckled at his own paranoia and lifted his mug in a mock toast to his reflection.

"Here's to you losing your mind, Borden," he said with a grin.

He took a sip.

He stopped.

The reflection did not.

THE SOUND of porcelain shattering on the floor echoed through the hallway as Borden stumbled back in shock, dropping his mug and letting out a frustrated groan. His reflection, which had been drinking the tea, continued to overflow with liquid until it spilled out of the mirror and onto the floor.

He directed his attention back up to the mirror, but it was no longer there.

A Blank wall?

It was as if the mirror had vanished. Frustrated, he turned around and let out a loud exhale, only to be startled by his own reflection in the mirror. It was a normal reflection, but Borden didn't expect it to be there. He waved and made gestures to confirm that it was just a regular mirror.

"Okay, I'm definitely not crazy. This mirror just switched sides."

Looking down at the remnants of the porcelain mug, he realized it belonged to Olivia.

"Shit, Olivia is gonna be pissed." He said to himself.

BORDEN DIDN'T REMEMBER ROTATING, but everything around him seemed to have a different idea. The entire hallway had undergone a complete reconfiguration. The door to his office, which was always on the left, had now moved to the right side, and even the picture on the wall had shifted.

It was as if the entire hallway had become a mirrored version of itself, starting with the disappearance and reappearance of the mirror.

As he stood in front of the placed office door, he felt unnerved.

"This can't be right," he said to himself, his words echoing through the empty hallway.

He shook his head, trying to rattle off the sense of disorientation that was settling in. The headaches started again, a dull ache that was nothing like the sharp pain from earlier.

Distracted, he tried to find a logical explanation for the strange turn of events. He remembered the house remodel they did a year ago, how they had rearranged the furniture and repainted the walls.

"That door used to be on the left," he called, trying to convince himself that his memory was playing tricks on him.

Maybe I'm just remembering it as it used to be.

. . .

He walked into his office and approached his desk, eager to work on his novel. As he sat down and booted up his computer, he hoped it would cooperate today.

"Come on, let's see if you want to work correctly today," he said under his breath, hoping to coax the machine into functioning.

As the computer booted up, he swiveled his chair back to the desk and prepared to start his work. But the strange occurrences he has experienced still distracted his mind. He took a deep breath and tried to focus on his writing, pushing aside the nagging doubts in his head.

Upon opening his computer, he navigated to a folder titled "Olivia_photos" on his desktop. As he clicked it open, an abundance of pictures emerged on the screen. He had perused this gallery many times before, especially when he felt distant from Olivia or when he longed for her company. The pictures stir romantic emotions within him, prompting his creative energy to flow. He closed the folder and launched the word processor, ready to type his love story.

He typed a few sentences, trying to capture the inspiration he had earlier. But the words didn't flow as easily as he'd hoped. He paused, staring at the blank page, feeling frustrated and stuck.

He heard a faint sound coming from outside the office. It was a soft whisper. But it was gone as quickly as it came.

He rubbed his eyes, wondering if he was just imagining things. Maybe he was just tired and overthinking everything.

Alright, let's do this. What's the theme–or better yet, the archetype?

He wasn't an expert in writing, but he knew the typical

structures that most novels followed. At the core of these stories, they all adhered to one of several archetypes.

"Overcoming the monster," he said to himself.

That could work.

This archetype followed the protagonist as they surmount an obstacle that seems insurmountable. He realized that the "monster" wouldn't be literal in his story. Instead, it could be something abstract, like time itself.

Time can appear monstrous in the lives of Olivia and Borden. Losing time was a crucial task they must overcome to stay together. The idea of time being the culprit responsible for the two lovers being apart intrigued Borden. He began:

> Two lovers; time has placed them together, but time has also kept them apart. There's a popular phrase like 'right place, right time. On the other side of that coin is also the "wrong place, wrong time."

He erased what he wrote. It was stupid. He typed a few new sentences, then deleted them. It was a familiar cycle that he'd been through before. He let out a frustrated sigh and caressed his chin.

But then he glimpsed the picture of Olivia on his desk and something inside him redirected. He remembered the love and support he's received from Olivia, and he knew she believed in him.

Borden realized that the real monster he needed to overcome was his own self-doubt. He needed to learn to love and believe in himself, just like Olivia did. And with that realization, he started typing again.

Nevertheless, he felt trapped in a cage, which only intensified after he became unemployed. It was as if he had become an overgrown hamster, with certain compartments in his cage meant for entertainment. The TV had become his hamster wheel. At least when he had a job, he felt like a hamster with a purpose.

Despite Olivia's reminders and reassurances, Borden couldn't ignore the inadequacy he felt. Being between jobs made him feel like he had lost his purpose in life. He couldn't help but question what life was without a sense of direction. Yes, creating a loving environment with Olivia was important to him, but he couldn't help but feel he was capable of more. He yearned for a greater purpose, something bigger than himself, to which he could contribute.

ON ONE PARTICULAR OCCASION, Borden had ordered some food. When it arrived, the driver approached the door and asked for confirmation of his order.

"Hi, for Burden?"

"Borden. With an 'or' sound. Borden."

The driver let off an embarrassed chuckle. It was a simple misunderstanding, but it stung. Borden's mind found it fitting. Borden the burden.

His self-given nickname had been bothering him for days until Olivia noticed that something was off. When he told her about it, she laughed. Not because she believed it to be true, but because of how close the words were and how easy the mistake was to make. She found it surprising that it had never happened before and even thought it could have been a childhood nickname of his.

Borden couldn't help but feel amazed by Olivia's kindness and love for him. Sometimes he wondered how he got so lucky to end up with someone so caring and considerate. Her heart of gold was one of a kind. Without Olivia, Borden would be lost. Her words of reassurance helped him realize he was overthinking the situation and that he was far from being an actual burden. To Olivia, he would never be that.

While Olivia is very caring and considerate, she has her moments of anger. Borden knew he has been quite the troublemaker in the house, and they have had many arguments over things that seem so trivial. One time, Olivia had asked him to pick up some fat-free milk from the grocery store, but he couldn't find it, so he ended up coming home with 1% milk instead. Olivia fought him with 100% of her might when he returned with the wrong carton of milk.

That was the extent of their arguments, thankfully. They never had to deal with anything serious like infidelity or betrayal, but for Olivia, the milk situation felt like a betrayal.

These memories of Olivia remind him of the interaction he had the night in the dirty kitchen.

She must have been fuming at how dirty it was!

He laughed.

That's odd. She called me 'Borden' instead of 'Angier'. She always calls me that when she's mad.

As Borden pondered over this detail, his mind wandered to other instances where Olivia called him by his last name during a heated argument.

It never came up.

She had reserved Angier for moments of annoyance, frustration, or anger. Why had she called him by his last name that night? Was it just a slip of the tongue, or was there something else behind it?

It was just used on official documents or when he was at a doctor's appointment. Even his mother-in-law referred to him as Angi, a shortened version of his name that she used as a term of endearment. She liked the name

Angi because it reminded her of angels. Borden found it interesting that someone who worked in the medical field could be so religious. He is not religious and thought it was more rational for doctors and nurses to rely on science and logic.

Nevertheless, he respects Mariana's beliefs and has never tried to challenge or change them. It was a two-way street, as Mariana knew Borden didn't share her religious views. Mariana would, however, prod Borden about the lack of effort in giving her a grandchild.

Borden, with his playful demeanor, always deflected the conversation, joking that Olivia was trouble enough in the house. Olivia would allow them to banter, recognizing that it's best not to interfere when they got riled up with each other.

As Borden recalled his past interactions with Olivia, he became more certain about his suspicions regarding her recent behavior. However, he also acknowledged that he has been acting strangely lately and that Olivia's behavior may be another strange occurrence in his life. While she may be an outlier in this situation, Borden couldn't ignore the possibility that something was amiss.

He accepted what he was about to do was beyond absurd, but he couldn't help himself.

It's going in the journal, no matter how crazy it seems.

Borden was surprised at himself. He was actually using the journal. Borden knew himself well enough to know that he would slowly stop using it until it became just another ancient artifact collecting dust.

But something about Olivia's strange behavior brought him back to it. With her voice echoing in his head, he grabbed the pen and wrote out a question with a harsh underline:

"Borden. Why did she call me Borden?"

The sight of his wife's name in the journal filled with absurd stories of monsters and supernatural events made Borden feel foolish. How could a sentence about his wife intertwine with stories about decaying planets and creatures?

This is stupid. Lucid dreams. And one minor inconsistency. That's all this is. No, I can't. This is going to jeopardize the integrity of whatever this journal is supposed to be.

He scratched out the previous question he wrote about Olivia. However, he remembered the incident with the hallway mirror and jotted it down in the journal:

"I still can't explain what happened in the hallway with the mirror. I remember feeling dizzy and seeing something move behind me, but when I turned around, there was nothing there. Then, when I looked back at my reflection, it was still drinking from the mug even though I had stopped. It was like I was seeing someone else in the mirror. And when I dropped the mug in shock, it shattered into a million pieces. Before that, I distinctly remember feeling a strange sensation when I touched the mirror. It was almost as if my hand went through it as if it were made of water or some other liquid substance. The experience was reminiscent of a sci-fi movie, like a portal into another dimension. Stupid. Olivia is gonna be pissed about that. That was her favorite mug.

My lack of sleep and poor nutrition, coupled with my overall declining health, has been taking its toll on me. I can't help

but feel like I belong among the corpses I dreamt about - maybe their deterioration is ahead of mine. The constant migraines only add to the chaos in my mind. I'm losing it, and I know I should probably talk to Olivia about it. But none of this explains what happened with the mirror in the hallway.

I can only assume that something is happening. The migraines could be the catalyst or perhaps a warning that something is off. It feels like a premonition like something is about to occur."

Borden had always found entertainment in watching horror films, laughing at the predictable jump scares and cheesy special effects. But now, as he reflected on the strange occurrences happening in his own life, he couldn't help but feel a sense of unease. Was this the direction his life was heading toward, becoming a character in his own horror movie? He wondered if it would be a good horror movie, with a satisfying resolution and a happy ending, or a bad one, where the protagonist met a gruesome fate. The uncertainty added to his growing anxiety.

Borden closed the journal and rested his hand on the cover, reflecting on what he had just written. It sounded crazy, but something was exciting about it. It felt like solving a case, an itch he could actually scratch. He hadn't felt that way in a while. Even if it meant his impending doom, he liked the feeling.

"What are you smiling about?" Olivia asked as she came through the archway dividing the kitchen and the living room.

"You're home!" he called.

He got up to kiss her. She noticed the journal.

"What's that?" she asked.

"Oh, nothing. I'm working on a brief experiment. I'm journaling. Dreams and stuff..."

He didn't want to make it a big deal or anything. He didn't like feeling patronized, even if he knew she meant well.

"Journaling. Fun. Is your little mishap about falling through the ceiling there?" she asked jokingly.

"It is. Sorry about the dirt."

Borden placed the journal on the coffee table.

"Dirt? Oh no, that was actually me. I forgot I was transferring over a plant into a new pot and it accidentally fell and spilled all over," she said as her voice trailed off, walking into the kitchen.

Borden is left puzzled.

"You did? Okay, that makes sense, I guess."

Borden couldn't avoid the feeling that something was off. Olivia's explanation for the dirt didn't quite add up, but he didn't want to push the issue. Borden waited for Olivia to move out of earshot before he picked up the journal again.

He wrote:

"Okay, this is weird now. Why did she say that? Why did she just openly lie to me? That's not even the weird part. Why lie about that? What does she gain by lying about the dirt in the kitchen?

Maybe she realized I had a moment of blacking out and she wants to spare me the embarrassment about it? That has to be it.

The problem with that is, I was conscious for a second or two after the 'fall' in that dream. I saw the dirt. It fell on my face as the hole sealed up. The dirt was there before she even got there. Why is she lying?"

Glancing towards the kitchen, Borden checked to see if Olivia was still busy, giving him a moment to focus on his thoughts without being interrupted.

She's busy.

Borden felt conflicted. Was it ethical to scrutinize Olivia's behavior over the next few days without her knowledge? He had planned on talking to her about the dreams, but with this new information, he decided to keep it to himself for the time being.

He rationalized that as long as his intentions were good; it was okay to scrutinize her. Something was definitely not right, and he needed to figure out what it was. As he finished his thoughts, he heard Olivia's footsteps approaching.

"Wow, you're really into that, huh?" she said sarcastically.

He snapped the journal shut and set it down.

"That's suspicious." She remarked.

"It's something silly, really. I probably won't use it much longer. You know how I am with those things."

He grinned with his arms expressively opened.

As Borden looked up at Olivia, he braced himself for a sarcastic remark about his "planner" obsession. But instead of a witty response, she looked at him with a blank expression. Her lack of reaction left him feeling stunned, yet some part of him had expected it.

It seemed like everything lately had been a series of inconsistencies, with no logical pattern or explanation. Silence filled the room as she stared at him without a word.

Is she gonna say anything?

"Yes, of course. I know how you are with those things." Olivia said, walking away from the conversation.

Her smile and abrupt departure left him feeling even

more confused. There was a hesitation in her reply that seemed uncharacteristic of her. It almost felt like she didn't believe her own words.

Borden paused and breathed deeply, trying to clear his head. He could feel the weight of the situation settling on his shoulders. This was no longer a matter of a fictional novel, it was real life. He couldn't ignore it or dismiss it as a figment of his imagination any longer.

With a newfound determination, Borden picked up the journal for the third time. He flipped through the pages, re-reading the accounts of his dreams and the strange occurrences around the house. He needed to approach this situation with a clear and level head.

As he read, he noticed the details were becoming more and more fantastical. Witchcraft, supernatural forces...it's all sounding like something out of a horror movie. Borden laughed nervously at the thought of Olivia being a witch. He knew he was getting carried away with his thoughts, but he couldn't help it.

Finally, he put a stop to it.

No novel for now. This is my project. Something's weird around here.

The journal would be his guide, and he would approach the situation with a logical mind. Borden was determined to sort this out, and he would not stop until he did.

As much as he disliked thinking about it, the rational conclusion was a hard pill to swallow.

He wondered if her behavior was a sign that she was hiding something from him, or if she was simply losing interest.

He has noticed her leaving early in the morning and coming home late at night more frequently, and staying out later. And she doesn't wear the watch he gifted her anymore, which he found concerning.

Demons and ghosts may be nonsense, but the strange occurrences happening around Borden were very real. He knew that his obsession with finding answers may lead to losing the one thing that is real and important to him - his love for Olivia.

Perhaps he has already lost her without realizing it. What started as a quest for finding logic in the irrational has turned into a dangerous obsession that threatens to consume him.

4

THE NURSE AND HOOD ORNAMENT

The violent pop of the truck's hood obscured the driver's vision, leaving him hurtling down the road toward an uncertain fate.

Borden and Olivia seized the moment, sitting together at their small dining table, sufficient for up to four people. However, they never needed the fourth chair, since Mariana, at most, would be the third at the table.

Each of them has their designated seat, not because they imposed it on themselves, but because they gravitated towards a particular spot. Much like when Borden slept on the left side of Olivia when they first shared a bed, it became his permanent spot for the rest of his life.

As Borden chewed on his toast, a curious expression crept onto his face. Olivia caught his glance and reciprocated. He smiled at her whenever their eyes met and altered his expression when she took a bite of her scrambled eggs.

Borden spoke with his mouth full of toast, crumbs falling from his lips as he said, "This is nice, right?"

Olivia nodded in agreement and replied, "Yes, it is."

Borden paused mid-bite, his eyes fixed on Olivia as if he was pondering something important. He swallowed his food and leaned back in his chair.

Interesting.

Borden looked up from his breakfast.

"You're not at work today?" he asked.

Olivia shook her head.

"We're short-staffed," she said, taking a bite of toast.

Borden nodded, but the tension between them was tangible.

"You always go above and beyond," he said, trying to keep the conversation light.

Olivia gave a clipped response.

"I don't have a choice, Borden," she said.

She broke apart another piece of toast, avoiding eye contact.

Borden cleared his throat and shifted his focus to Olivia, his gaze intense.

"I'm just saying that sometimes we have to make tough choices, and I hope we're doing what's best for us," he said with a hint of frustration.

Olivia looked up from her plate, sensing the passive aggressiveness in his tone.

"I don't understand what you're trying to say," she said, her annoyance mounting.

Borden wiped his mouth with a napkin. He rearranged the dishes in front of him, creating space for his elbows. He leaned forward, assuming an inquisitive posture.

"Why are you sitting there?" he asked, "Specifically, in that chair?"

"I don't understand why that matters."

"That's Mariana's spot."

Olivia expressed surprise as she said, "Mariana?"

Borden's eyebrow arched at Olivia's response.

"Mariana, yes, my mom. I remember." Olivia said, sensing Borden's confusion.

"You never sit there, and you would question me had I been one to sit in the wrong chair," Borden said, pointing over at the fourth chair they never use.

"Yeah, you're right. Of course. I forgot, I guess. I'm just stressed out. From work." Olivia said, bowing her head in an exhausted fashion.

"I'm sorry. I know you must be."

Borden realized the gravity of the situation and backed off, adopting a friendlier and more welcoming demeanor. He had gotten the information he needed, and there was no point in further antagonizing Olivia.

He realized this moment was being jeopardized by his personal and hidden agenda.

As he gazed at her face, the softness of her features struck him. Memories of the girl he once proposed to inhabit his mind, and he remembered his desire to make her the happiest person on earth. Meanwhile, she cleaned up her side of the table.

Time seemed to slow down, bending to their will. The beauty and peace within this frame of thought were clear as if they were living inside a Polaroid picture. Every passing minute should feel precious and filled with love. Petty quarrels were pointless in the face of such precious time. Of course, every couple, every friend, will have their disagreements. These moments are opportunities for clashing opinions to settle into a new understanding, leading to deeper levels of connection.

Understanding was at the core of their true love. The ability to comprehend each other kept them sane. They knew each other to the nth degree, down to the minute details, including flaws, quirks, triggers, preferences, and body language.

Borden had a hard time accepting how he ended up with someone who could read him like a book. Countless times they have spent evenings at events, communicating with a simple shift in body weight. The two of them were connected on a deeper level, guided by the laws of attraction.

"Hello? Is anybody there? Borden honey," Olivia said.

Borden snapped out of it.

"I was just thinking–"

"Of what?"

"Us, you know," Borden said.

"Oh, yeah?"

"I just find it interesting that–," Borden said, pausing before his next statement.

After a moment of hesitation, Borden looked up to confront her about the line of questioning that she had failed, only to realize that sitting next to her was a faceless nurse. He froze in terror, his eyes locked on the featureless figure.

"Olivia?" He asked, stuttering as he pointed at the figure.

"What?" She asked.

The faceless nurse jerked her head directly at Borden.

He shrieked in terror, falling out of his chair.

"Borden! What's wrong?" Olivia shouted.

"Olivia! There's someone there!"

His voice trembled with panic as he pleaded with Olivia, too afraid to look over the table.

"Don't you see her? Please tell me you do!" he called out.

"Borden, get up. There's no one here."

Borden, trusting her word, lifted the tablecloth to take a peak underneath.

"Olivia! I see someone's legs next to yours! I'm dreaming again. Damn it! I'm dreaming again!"

"Borden, you're not dreaming, but there isn't anyone here. What's the matter with you?"

Borden remained on the floor, trembling with fear and repeating to himself to wake up.

Olivia was now worried and demanded an explanation. However, Borden cannot articulate anything, and his headache was only getting worse. The room felt like it was shrinking, and the walls began to close in on him, making it hard for him to breathe.

Something's going to happen. What is it?

As Borden lay there, he felt the weight of the universe pressing down on him. The emptiness was suffocating. He tried to scream, but no sound escaped his lips. It was as if they had trapped him in a vacuum-sealed container with nothing but his thoughts.

Every passing second felt like an eternity as he struggled to come to terms with what was happening. He had never felt so alone, so isolated from the rest of the world. At that moment, he realized he was powerless, at the mercy of the universe.

Before him was the dining table.

And nothing more.

"Olivia?" He asked.

But it was only him now, and the table in front of him.

Borden fixated his eyes on the tablecloth as a head of hair emerged from it. He was terrified but unable to look away. The nurse who had been sitting next to Olivia crawled out from underneath the tablecloth.

Borden prepared to scream, but the nurse's hand silenced him.

"Shh," she said, her voice echoing in the space.

With one hand on Borden's mouth, she raised the other hand and pointed to where Olivia once stood. Borden's eyes followed her gesture and understood the message she was conveying. His eyes tried to communicate what his silenced voice wanted to say, *Who is she?*

The nurse ominously shook her head, moving it from left to right. Her hand slid down his lips and came to a stop on his chest.

Borden's mouth was free, and he expected to scream, but now his ears were eager to hear what she had to say.

"Go back," the nurse's harrowing voice reverberated in his head.

"Go back where?" Borden asked.

"Not here. Not yet," the nurse said, shaking her head and gesturing towards the table.

Borden, puzzled, asked, "What do you mean?"

Borden couldn't make out any distinct details of the nurse's distorted face.

"She's not–"

Borden's stomach dropped.

"She's not what?" He asked.

THE WORLD AROUND HIM TREMBLED. Brick by brick, the house began reconstructing, the walls lifting from the ground.

"She's not what?" He chanted.

Something had brought his kitchen back, and it swept away the nurse under the tablecloth.

"No, no! She's not what?" Borden called out, crawling towards the tablecloth.

"Borden!" Olivia called, watching her husband searching around the kitchen.

Borden raised the cloth but found no one underneath. He looked around the table, but there was still no sign of the nurse.

"Borden, talk to me!" Olivia announced, growing worried.

Borden appeared to be in a trance-like state, searching for answers. He ignored Olivia's attempts to communicate with him, muttering to himself instead.

"Where is she? Where did she go?"

"There's no one here. What are you talking about?" Olivia asked. "You're not well, Borden. First the dream, and now this?"

Despite her concern, Olivia attempted to see what Borden did, but she saw nothing unusual.

Borden spoke, disturbingly admitting, "She didn't have a face."

I sound crazy. What am I even saying? Look at her, she's horrified. Not from what I saw, but from what I told her.

Olivia tried to offer some words of support, hoping to calm Borden down and move on from the unsettling experience. However, Borden remained overwhelmed, lost in his thoughts once more. He just can't catch a break.

I need to add that to the journal.

Olivia stared down at Borden, a worried look on her face.

"Maybe we should talk about our upcoming trip." She said.

"Trip? What do you mean by trip?" He asked.

Borden realized he hasn't been keeping track of time and that the trip was approaching quickly.

"Why are we even talking about the trip? Did you not hear what just happened? I don't think I even want to go, not like this. I'm in no shape for traveling."

Olivia looked displeased. Bothered.

"Well, Borden, we're going, and that's final," she said. She stood and exited the kitchen.

"Yeah, of course, run off to work!"

Olivia grabbed her belongings and stormed out.

Borden sat alone at the table, seething with anger. He couldn't believe that Olivia lied to him again. Instead of feeling sad or guilty about the argument they just had, he's upset that he couldn't trust her. Borden was done with the secrecy.

I can't believe she failed that test.

When he asked about the seat, she hesitated and claimed to have forgotten. Borden had let that slide.

That was a valid mistake.

He got her to admit that she, too, would have made a big deal out of him sitting in the wrong chair. That was the funny part. He was sitting in the wrong chair from the start. He never admitted to that fact, and it was a test within a test. Olivia failed both tests. More and more inconsistencies.

Olivia steered with one hand and pressed the other against her forehead, overcome with emotion as she drove toward the hospital. She pulled over, turned off the engine, and gripped the car keys. Her keychain featured a birthstone that Borden gave her as a good luck charm, and she clutched it to her chest as tears streamed down her face. Just like the cars on the road, life kept moving forward.

When she pulled down the windshield sunshade, she saw a Polaroid picture of Borden which only intensified her sorrow.

What's wrong with you Borden? What can I do to help you? I'm trying everything I can. Nothing seems to help. I don't want us to fall apart. You and I, we're connected. Talk to me. I'm trying.

Using her sleeves, she wiped away the tears. She looked at herself in the rearview mirror, took a deep breath, and turned the car back on. Checking for oncoming traffic once more in the rearview mirror, she pulled out onto the road.

"Ah!" she screamed.

For a split second, someone was visible in the mirror's reflection.

She removed her seatbelt and rushed out of the car. There was no one in it. She didn't see anyone in the backseat.

"I swear I"—

Olivia turned pale.

"That's a-a-a-face," she said.

THE THUNDERING SOUND of metal slamming against metal echoed through the air as the hood of a truck popped up. The hood obscured the driver's vision, leaving him hurtling down the road toward an uncertain fate.

Olivia was still in a trance, stuck in fear. Someone was breathing into the rear passenger window. Watching it write with its finger. Its breath took turns to allow for more space to write.

The screech of the truck's brakes filled the air as the heavy vehicle skidded along the rough asphalt road, its tires leaving behind a trail of smoke and debris.

The finger continued to slide along the window.

She tried to make out the words.

Let...

Him...

The truck's hood came down with a loud bang, as if by some divine intervention.

"Go," Olivia said, snapping out of her trance-like state and screaming at the sight of the truck hurtling toward her.

The loud screeching of brakes and the acrid smell of burned rubber overwhelmed her. The truck skidded to a stop just inches from her face. The enormous vehicle hung over her like a menacing monster.

The hood ornament stared at her. The heat from the engine warmed her up to reality. Shaking, she looked over at her car. It was empty.

"Holy shit, lady, you alright?" A stumbling man said, exiting his truck. "What are you doing on the road? Are you crazy or something?"

The man was in shock. He frightened himself as well.

"My hood flew up and I couldn't see anything. It's a damn miracle I didn't hit ya!"

Olivia was still struggling to catch her breath, unable to process the idea of death and the horror of what she had just witnessed.

"Are you okay? Do you need help?" he asked, concerned about her mental health.

"What, yeah. Sorry, I'm okay. I just–" she said.

"You sure? Do you need a ride or something?" he asked.

"No, I have a car, thank you," she said, pointing over at her pulled-over car off the road.

"Flat tire or what?"

"No, I was just taking a break."

Everything that was happening puzzled the man. Despite his offer of help, she declined it, leaving him feeling relieved of his moral obligation.

"Okay, just be careful, please. Get home safe," he called, entering his vehicle.

He pulled out around her and drove off.

Olivia made her way off the road to the shoulder. Now that the highway was empty, she hesitated before entering her car, checking the backseat for the millionth time before proceeding inside.

After firing up the engine, she adjusted her rearview mirror and angled it towards the back for a second, but saw nothing and no one. She adjusted it back to its normal position, took a deep breath, and made her way back onto the highway.

Let him go.

Let him go?

The hospital was still several miles away, so the silent cabin allowed her to gather her thoughts.

What could that mean? A bad omen?

Despite their contrasting views on the supernatural, she and Borden had always enjoyed a good scare. She shared her mother's fascination with the spiritual world, while Borden found amusement in horror films that she took seriously. She acknowledged the movies were fictional, yet the subject still made her uneasy.

One Halloween, Borden took their fascination with the unknown to a new level by bringing out a Ouija board. He found communicating with ghosts through plywood and the alphabet hilarious, but soon realized his mistake. The experience left her shaken, and Borden learned to try nothing like that again. If he did, he might need a Ouija board just to communicate with her.

After taking a moment to compose herself, she pulled into her reserved parking space at the hospital. A sign with her name on it greeted her as she gathered her things and stepped out of the car. She drew in a big breath, filling her lungs with the cool air.

Although she dreaded the days when a patient wouldn't make it, there was still a sense of excitement that pulsed through her veins as she entered the hospital. She took comfort in the familiar sights and sounds - the squeak of sneakers on linoleum floors, the beep of monitors, and the steady hum of the ventilation system.

Having said that, a part of her didn't want to be there.

The building, once her sanctuary, had become a place of heartbreak and tragedy.

Olivia stopped in front of the automatic doors before walking inside. She looked at her parked car in effort to see what she saw on the road. But it was empty.

I'm losing my mind.

5

VANILLA PUDDING

There was an emergency at the hospital, and Olivia was urgently requested to be there. The patient in Room D had unexplained seizures.

Back home, Borden sat in his office, pen in hand and a journal in front of him. With fabricated courage, he said out loud, "Nurse, are you there?"

Clack!

What was that?

A creak made him wonder. He reassured himself that it was just the typical noises an old house makes - plumbing or walls expanding. Borden then read over his notes in the journal and categorized them into a list of supernatural experiences and Olivia's strange behavior. He wrote:

"Supernatural Stuff"

- **Graveyard 'dream' - Ghouls talking to me**
- **The laptop 'communicating with me,' 'Hi Borden,'**
- **The mirror, what is that mirror? That reflection also? I don't even remember having that mirror in the house. It appeared behind me. I know it. I don't have vertigo. I had overlooked the door in the remodel.**
- **The nurse. This goddamn nurse. I'm not crazy. Olivia was there for this one too, but she didn't see her. 'She's not...' What did she try to say? She pointed at Olivia.**

"Am I just fucked up? Maybe it is all in my head. Maybe they're all crazy manifestations of my own insecurities. The ghouls telling me that 'I don't belong' sounds like my subconscious telling me I don't belong in this house. In this relationship. That I'm not good enough. I don't know. But then, what did 'it's too late for us' mean? Too late for reconciliation, perhaps?"

He moved lower on the page and made a list for Olivia. Although it didn't feel right, he felt compelled to do so because everything seemed to be connected, even if he no longer felt connected to her. He wrote:

"Olivia"

- **She lied about the dirt. Whether she protected me from shame or embarrassment, she lied. That's unusual.**
- **I almost forgot about this, but, about the dirt, I recall having a dream or I don't know if it was from being half-awake, but I swear I saw her**

eating the dirt. This sounds so stupid, but it falls under her being strange. Dream or not. I need to put everything on the table.

- **She's always gone. I know she has long shifts, but every time I'm awake or need her, she's not home.**
- **She called me 'Borden' instead of 'Angier' and that's just out of character. She was mad.**
- **She pretended to 'know me' when I mentioned the journal, another form of lying, or at least, concealing something from me.**
- **She keeps mentioning this trip, that I don't want to be a part of. I don't know where we're going, she just says I'll like it there.**
- **Are we not as connected as I thought we were? Olivia used to know what I was thinking, what I was feeling just by resting my head on her lap. No matter where we were, we'd be able to communicate somehow. I guess not.**
- **The chairs. The musical chairs. I joke, but that was a trap that I didn't expect to work. I hate that it worked."**

Borden's hands trembled as he scanned his two lists. He let out a deep sigh and slumped in his chair as he realized that investigating Olivia's list made him feel more uneasy than the idea of tackling the supernatural one. So far, the only negative consequence of the supernatural experiences had been the headaches, and Borden had suffered no notable harm from them. Olivia, on the other hand, had been hurtful to him.

. . .

THE LIGHTS FLICKERED ONCE, twice, and then again, more persistently. Borden's grip on the journal tightened as his senses sharpened. He could feel his heartbeat quickening and his breath becoming shallow. Something was happening.

He tried to push down the rising feeling of anxiety and repeated to himself, "Stay alert, Borden."

Borden lost his balance as the entire house rumbled. Panic set in as he realized it was an earthquake. He ran under the doorframe, avoiding objects falling off the walls. Terrified, he cowered, waiting for the shaking to stop. Once the earthquake subsided, Borden felt a sharp pain in his head, a migraine setting in.

Borden couldn't resist the excruciating migraine, and it consumed him like a dark, suffocating cloud. The pain throbbed behind his eyes, and he felt nauseous and dizzy. The world faded to black.

OLIVIA WAS TACKLING an emergency of her own over at the hospital. The patient in Room D was experiencing unexplained seizures. Upon hearing that the patient had stabilized, Olivia gave instructions to the nurses before moving on to her next patient in room B.

The woman in the bed was much older than Olivia's mother, but she approached her with the same kindness and compassion she showed to all her patients. Olivia knew how to speak to them, offering words of comfort and encouragement to help them face the day ahead. She knew some doctors lack this trait, but she always strived to connect with her patients. Olivia loved the woman in Patient Room B.

"Hi Daisy, how are we feeling today?"

Daisy, a 72-year-old woman with a youthful spirit, turned to Olivia and said, "Hungry. Do we have any more of those vanilla puddings?"

The puddings were a popular treat among the patients, providing a welcome distraction from their exhaustion and pain.

"I think I might have a couple left. You might be in luck," Olivia said, winking at Daisy. "So you want two?" she confirmed.

"Why yes, if you insist. I'll have two," Daisy responded, her wrinkles crinkling with a smile.

Olivia smiled back and nodded. Daisy's toothless grin was endearing, but her eyes shared most of her joy these days. Daisy had been a regular patient at the hospital, and Olivia hoped this would be the last time she saw her there. Although Olivia loved having Daisy around, she knew she deserved to travel the world and enjoy life as much as possible.

"Did you say hi to your mother for me?" Daisy asked.

"Yes, of course! She hopes you're feeling better."

"I am. As long as I get those puddings."

DURING DAISY'S first hospital stay, Olivia's mom had taken care of her. Despite the time that had passed, Mariana's reminder to Olivia was always the same: "Remember the vanilla pudding."

OLIVIA HEADED to the cafeteria where people were walking back and forth, creating a lively atmosphere. The smell of grilled meats and hearty stews was so delicious that it could be mistaken for a five-star restaurant. Olivia greeted the cooks as she passed by, and they responded with courteous nods, making her feel special.

"Dr. Borden! How's it going?" the head chef shouted.

"Long day, Mario! Long day," she said, smiling.

"What do you need?" he asked.

"Pudding for Daisy. Vanilla."

"Here you go. How's your boy doing?"

"Growing. Like a weed," he said.

"Thanks, Mario."

Turning, she remembered she needed a second pudding and asked, "Sorry, may I have another one?"

"Of course."

As she picked up the second pudding, her gaze caught the reflection in the salad bar window. A figure resembling Borden caught her eye. She scanned the bustling cafeteria but saw no sign of the person in question.

"Mario, did you see someone standing behind me?"

"When?"

"Just now."

"No, I don't think so. Is someone looking for you?"

"No, never mind. Thanks again." Olivia said.

"Anytime."

Olivia made her way back to Patient Room B, her steps slow and deliberate. She paused at the entrance, her gaze shifting towards Patient Room C and D, located just across the hallway. A sense of foreboding crept up on her, and she made a mental note to check on them later.

Daisy's applause broke her from her reverie as she

walked into the room, holding the pudding. Daisy's joy was palpable, and Olivia couldn't help but feel a sense of relief. It was moments like these that made working at the hospital worthwhile, seeing the pleasure on her patients' faces for things that many of us take for granted. Despite her reservations, Olivia couldn't deny the pudding's deliciousness.

"Wonderful! Bring it here!" Daisy called out.

"I apologize. I could only get one serving of pudding for you," Olivia said, her tone apologetic.

"Ah, that's okay, dear," Daisy said with a smile.

"Just kidding! Here it is," Olivia said, presenting the pudding to Daisy.

"Haha, I knew you were pulling my leg, you mischievous rascal!" Daisy called out as she took the pudding from Olivia's hands.

DAISY DEVOURED the pudding like a ravenous beast, her eyes widening with delight. Olivia stood by, happy to see the joy on her patient's face.

"Is there anything else you need before I go?" Olivia asked, anticipating the usual request for a glass of water or a fluff of Daisy's pillows.

"Sleep. I'm ready for a nap," Daisy said, her voice soft and frail.

Olivia nodded, ready to leave, but before she could turn away, Daisy spoke up again. "How's Angi?"

"He's doing alright," Olivia said, trying to infuse some optimism into her voice. "I'm sure he'll have some better days soon."

Daisy smiled. "That's grand. I like him. He's sweet."

Olivia nodded in agreement and wished Daisy a peaceful rest.

A VICE-LIKE GRIP suddenly took hold of Olivia's wrist, causing her to gasp in pain.

"Daisy!" Olivia screamed, trying to pull her hand away.

But Daisy's grip was unyielding, and she looked up at Olivia with eyes rolled to white, the sclera stark against the crimson vessels.

"Let him go!"

Olivia screamed in terror as she tried to break free from the grip, but it only tightened, cutting off the circulation in her hand.

"Let go of me!" Olivia screamed again, struggling to break free.

The ominous grip of Daisy's fingers released, and her face returned to its previous frail and peaceful appearance. Olivia stood frightened in shock, her heart pounding in her chest.

"ARE YOU OKAY, DAISY?" she asked, her voice trembling.

Daisy's eyes fluttered open, and she smiled at Olivia. "Of course, dearie. Why do you ask?"

Olivia's mind raced, trying to make sense of what had just happened. "You...you grabbed my wrist and said something... strange," she said.

Daisy chuckled. "Oh, that. I must have been dreaming. I have vivid dreams sometimes."

Olivia nodded, still feeling unnerved. "Well, I'm glad you're okay now. Do you need anything else before I go?"

Daisy shook her head. "No, dearie. Thanks for the pudding. It was delicious."

Olivia forced a smile.

"You're welcome, Daisy. Rest well."

SHE WALKED out of the room, feeling speechless and devoid of thoughts and emotion. As she turned the corner, a man bumped into her, causing Olivia to excuse herself. She was still jittery from the encounter with Daisy. The man carried on with his pace, not bothering to acknowledge the collision. Olivia dismissed it, but then she recognized the scent that lingered in the air.

"That cologne?" she said to herself.

She turned her face towards him. But he was already far down the hall, mingling with the people who were traversing the hospital floors. Olivia kept her eyes fixed on the man as he walked out of the hospital. She started pacing towards him, which turned into a sprint.

That's the man from the salad bar, she thought.

Excusing herself and bumping into people along the way, Olivia raced to catch up to the man. She was not far behind him before he started disappearing into the crowds. She weaved through the throngs of people, trying to keep him in sight, but a stretcher blocked her path, forcing her to wait. As she watched him turn a corner in the distance, she realized it was too late - he was gone.

I could've sworn that was...no. It wasn't.

A nurse who had watched her run was worried that she was having an emergency. Olivia, looking defeated and winded from the chase, only added to the nurse's curiosity.

"Is something wrong, Doctor?" she asked.

"No, I'm fine," Olivia said, knowing that she most likely was not.

Back at home, after what seemed like hours, Borden woke up in a unique spot. This didn't surprise him too much, as he had a history of sleepwalking events. He recalled one sleepwalking moment and chuckled at the memory. However, Olivia didn't find it amusing.

Borden groggily climbed out of bed, stumbling over to the dresser and he used it as his commode. The sound of urine hitting the wood woke up Olivia. She bolted upright, her eyes wide with shock and confusion. "What are you doing?!" she yelled at him. "Angier! You're peeing on our dresser!"

This, he found out later, since he heard nothing she was saying to him. He hasn't had a similar experience, and he's thankful for that. He thought that was enough to end his marriage.

"Well, no weird dreams this time," he said, rubbing the back of his head and looking around at the aftermath of the earthquake. "Damn it, I need to clean this up. The television didn't fall, that's good."

He started with the large things first. Then he moved on to adjust any furniture that may have slid around a bit. He shifted the coffee table over and the leg got caught on the rug. He tugged on it before noticing and he heard a tear. Like paper. He paused and examined the tear on the rug. It was a small, jagged rip, about the size of a quarter.

What the hell?

He stooped down to investigate the floor. It appeared to be peeling, and he used his nail to pick at it, lifting more and more of it. "This is like wallpaper," he mused.

Growing more curious, he realized his finger won't be effective and ran over to the kitchen to fetch a spatula, thinking it might help him detach the peeling material more easily.

Running back to the wallpaper floor, he stopped.

Puzzled, he looks down.

It was right here, wasn't it?

He stooped down again for a closer look. His hand caressed the floor, confused why it looked normal.

"That's a good one, ghost-nurse, graveyard demons. Whatever is doing this..." he called out sarcastically.

HE STARTED PICKING up the objects that fell around the house. He made a pile for the things that didn't survive.

No, not that vase, damn it, Olivia loves that thing.

He held the vase in its pieces, thinking for a moment that with some glue and a bit of handiwork, he might have been able to puzzle it together. He grabbed a piece in each hand, trying to join them. But it was no use; the break was too clean, and the pieces didn't fit together. He set the pieces back down on the table, feeling frustrated.

A framed picture caught his attention as he scrambled for more broken items. He moved some debris out of the way and picked it up. Blowing on it to remove some collected dust, he inspected it.

"That's her! That's... yeah, that's her! It has to be. Same hair, same build. It has to be!" he called out, referring to the woman in the picture.

It was a picture of Olivia, taken at the hospital with some of her colleagues. Olivia stood in between her residents and some nurses, and on Olivia's left side, there she stood - the nurse who had appeared at his breakfast table.

She had no face, but I just know for a fact, this is her. Judging from her hair, it must be. I'll have to ask Olivia about it when she's back!

He placed the picture on the coffee table so he wouldn't forget to ask about it later.

DRIVING HOME, Olivia made a stop at Mariana's house. She didn't like the way their last conversation over the phone had gone. When she pulled up to the driveway, she knocked on the door. Mariana took a while to answer, as her house had two stories, and she wasn't as young as she used to be.

Olivia remembered telling Mariana when she bought the house that she would regret having stairs one day. Although not that day yet, it was getting there.

Knock Knock!

She knocked again.

Someone on the other side of the door emitted a quiet and muffled voice.

"I'm coming, I'm coming."

Olivia waited.

"Who is it?"

"It's me, ma."

She opened the door. The two looked at each other before embracing in each other's arms. Olivia had tears in her eyes, and her stressful day was apparent.

"There, there, Oli."

. . .

At that moment, Olivia was the eight-year-old little girl waiting for her mother to console her.

"Come on in, baby."

Mariana guided her into the house and closed the door.

6

A SEA OF CRIMSON

"Oh you don't like that? Poor big man needs his wife to take care of him. You want your Binky, Burden?"

A foreboding shadow loomed over the picture of Olivia and the nurse. Left on the table in the living room by Borden. a bright light glowed in the corner, illuminating the room. The light intensified, engulfing the picture in flames. The shadowy figure shifted along the walls, disappearing as it reached the hallway before reemerging in Borden's bedroom.

It crept toward his bed, its amorphous form taking shape over his body. With a sudden movement, the shadow disappeared, as if it has entered Borden's body through his very pores. Borden's eyes snapped open, and a shiver coursed through his body as he sensed an ominous presence within him.

Am I sleeping in a freezer? What is this?

Shivering, he clutched at the comforter to extract the most possible warmth from it.

"Olivia," he said.

No reply.

She's sleeping.

He lifted his comforter to adjust his body over to Olivia's.

As he shifted his leg over to her side, it was met with emptiness. More bed space. He threw the comforter away from his face, revealing the bed.

He was in it alone.

Olivia wasn't there.

"OLIVIA," he called out.

There was no response.

He rubbed his eyes and took a deep breath. He exhaled, sat upright, tossed his legs over the edge of the bed, and aligned his slippers for easy access. He flicked on his nightstand lamp, but it didn't agree with him.

Was this broken? Damn it. Nothing works.

He stepped outside of his bedroom. The hallway was pitch black. That portion of the house had no windows, so it was always dark. It also wasn't a very long hallway, so it wasn't a problem, anyway. The light switch for the living room was just seven feet away from his bedroom.

That's odd. Where's the light switch?

Although he couldn't see, Borden continued walking, with the muscle memory of doing it for years. After more than a few steps, he reached out his hand to find the light switch, but there was nothing there. He kept walking, growing annoyed at what felt like a parlor trick.

Am I on a fucking treadmill?

Borden snapped out of the half-awake zombie he was and started walking faster. He started running. Only darkness surrounded him. He glanced back, yet the same destiny that awaited him was still present. Pure darkness. The air was frosty, and a putrid smell filled his nostrils. He could hear his breathing, a loud inhale and exhale that echoed in the empty hallway. Every step he took made a soft thud on the ground, but the sound felt hollow.

"This way, Borden," a ghastly voice said in the night's stillness.

"Who's there?" his voice trembled, failing to mask his fright.

"This way, Borden," the voice said.

Borden hesitated, feeling unsure and vulnerable. He knew he had no other choice since he couldn't see anything, anyway. With a deep breath, he raised his hands in front of him and continued walking.

"Where are we going?" he asked.

No response.

Step by step.

He rubbed his hands together for warmth.

"Here," the voice finally called out.

Borden reached out and felt a switch. He flicked it. Blinded at first by the light, he covered his eyes with his arm. Once the brightness settled, he lowered his arm.

"**AH!**"

Borden let out a massive shout before a scowl replaced his fright.

The hallway mirror, face to face with Borden, startled him with his reflection.

This thing again, no, no, this mirror–something wasn't right!

Borden's heart raced as he grabbed the mirror, his fingers trembling with urgency and desperation. He clutched it close to his chest and darted towards his office, his feet pounding against the hardwood floor.

Once inside, he slammed the door shut and locked it. His hands were shaking as he placed the mirror on his desk. He paced back and forth, his mind filled with questions and fears.

What was happening to him? Why was he seeing things that weren't there? Was he losing his mind? He needed answers, and he needed them fast.

"Hey, voice, are you still here?" he screamed in desperation.

"Why'd you lead me to this thing?"

No reply.

"Hello!"

A MOCKING SILENCE. Borden was beyond frustrated by then. He removed a frame from the wall and replaced it with the mirror.

Borden studied the mirror, arms crossed, staring at his reflection.

"Why was I led to this? We've never had this mirror in the house. I know it. Where did it come from? Why is it important?" he wondered.

As he reached out with his finger, he felt a cool, smooth surface beneath it. The glass seemed to vibrate, sending shivers down his spine. The ripples on the surface grew larger and more intense as if the mirror were alive and breathing. His curiosity and desperation got the better of him. He pressed his finger against the glass, and as he did, he felt a sudden jolt, as if he had touched an electric wire. The mirror shook violently, and a bright light filled the room.

As his finger contacted the glass, a ripple effect emanated from the point of contact, creating concentric rings that expanded outwardly. The intensity of the light emanating from the mirror increased, blinding Borden momentarily. He couldn't explain it, but the effect he was witnessing was magical.

Borden felt a strange magnetic aura pulling him toward the mirror. The more he fought against it, the stronger the force became. His body was now being sucked into the mirror, inch by inch, and he couldn't seem to resist its power. The glass glowed with its blinding light, and he heard a distant voice calling out to him from the depths of the mirror. Desperate to break free, Borden screamed for help, but no one was around to hear him.

The water currents swelled with intensity, and he felt an invisible force pull him deeper and deeper into the depths. He attempted to fight against the frame, but the water currents were too powerful.

Borden's office was now empty, with only a mirror on the wall that had returned to its normal state. The water that was once swirling inside it now dripped along the wall, cascading down to form a puddle on the ground. Borden was gone.

Caught in a riptide, the weight of the deep waters crushed Borden. He oriented himself to look upwards towards the surface, but all he could see was the blood-stained hue of the water. The mysterious current spun and spat out

Borden close to drowning. Coughing out water and struggling to stay afloat, he turned as he paddled with his feet, trying to get a sense of his surroundings.

To his horror, he realized he was no longer in his world. The entire ocean was red, an alien and surreal environment.

Where am I?

Borden asked himself if he was bleeding, but he wasn't. The water just wasn't the blue he was used to. The deep, crimson-red color of the water was so unexpected that it took him aback.

"It's red. Like blood! This can't be real. Olivia's going to find me on the floor soon," he said to himself.

He spotted something in the distance, sails. It was a boat.

"That's a boat!" he howled, flailing his arms out of the water, attempting to make himself seen.

But the boat was too far and seemed to be headed in a different direction.

"Hey!" He continued to scream. "Over here!" gurgling water.

Something yanked Borden below the surface, enough for his head to go underwater and right back out.

What was that?

Borden rotated himself in the water, trying to look below the surface, but it was too hazy and dark. He couldn't keep this up forever. His arms were going to give out soon. So were his legs.

There was something down there. He had felt it before, and the feeling was growing stronger. It was an ominous presence, like a shadow lurking in the depths. The surrounding water swirled, and he felt himself being pulled downwards. Panic set in as he struggled against the invisible force.

His efforts returned to the boat.

"HEY!"

The sails, he thought. *They're turning! Right? Yes, yes, they are!*

The boat appeared to shift its course. The boat was turning around for Borden.

His ankle felt another tug.

"Shit!" he said as he spit out water. "Hurry!"

The boat grew in size. It's getting closer to Borden.

"Hurry!"

Borden noticed something odd about the boat. It was like nothing he had ever seen before. The design was sleek, and it shone with a glossy finish that made it look like something from the future. But what was even more strange was the way it moved across the water. It didn't seem to contact the water at all. Instead, it glided effortlessly above it, leaving no trace behind.

It filled Borden with a mix of awe and fear at the sight. He couldn't decide which fate seemed worse: getting on that boat or what awaited him beneath the water. But the decision was not his to make. It was too late. The water pulled him back under.

Borden's struggles only seemed to tighten the grip on his leg. He tried to kick free, but the grip was too strong.

He felt a sharp pain shoot through his leg, and he cried out in agony. His vision faded, and he felt himself losing consciousness.

"Olivia," he said, his voice trapped within an air bubble that burst as it reached the surface.

. . .

As he continued to descend, he noticed something glowing in the distance. It was faint at first, but it grew brighter as he got closer. The glow was coming from a cave, and Borden realized he was being pulled towards it.

Invisible tendrils, like the arms of a sea monster, wrapped around him and dragged him into the dark abyss. He passed through the bright light and the tendrils released him onto the hard ground of a cave.

The pressure of the water vanished, and he gasped for air, feeling the relief of being able to breathe again. Looking around, he saw a waterfall cascading down from the entrance they pulled him through, and the walls of the cave glowed with an eerie blue light.

"Where am I?" he asked, his voice echoing through the cavern.

As he caught his breath, the smell of formaldehyde hit him again, making him gag. He stood up and saw a corpse, similar to the ones from the graveyard. The stench was overpowering, creating a miasmic atmosphere that made it hard to focus.

"Why did you bring me down here?" Borden asked.

The decaying once-human looked at him. It gestured towards what was above them. "You, you shouldn't be here. You, you must go back," it said.

"Go back, where? Why shouldn't I be here?"

Annoyed, Borden said, "I'm tired of constantly hearing that and nothing more!"

Borden began feeling nauseated from the smell. His insides were making their way out.

"The boat. You, you shouldn't be here. You're not ready."

The creature lifted its bone-exposed limb towards an opening that appeared on the wall. It took the shape of a mirror, similar to the one in his office that brought him to this place. The mirror triggered the same effects, and the magnetic aura pulled Borden inside - a treacherous trick.

"Leave, you must leave. No Boat."

He called out for more answers, and the whirlpool engulfed his body once more, etched into the wall. He emerged from the mirror in his office. Borden collapsed onto the floor, his clothes soaking wet. He ran his hands through his hair and got to his feet. He looked back and met his reflection: a soaking Borden, panting.

This mirror. What are they trying to tell me?

He poked the mirror, hoping to trigger the ripples.

It's not working.

"The vague messengers are getting on my nerves," he said to himself. "They speak in goddamn riddles! Why can't they just tell me?"

In frustration, he knocked around the items on his desk and grabbed the journal.

"What the fuck is the point of this?" he howled at his reflection. He waited for an answer, but there was none. He felt like he was going insane.

"Huh! Well? What is it?"

He continued to yell, flipping open the journal in anger as if to show his reflection on what he had written. Then, he stopped screaming.

BORDEN, had a blank expression on his face, matching the blank contents of the journal. He flipped the pages.

Blank.

Blank.

Blank.

"What the hell? Where are my notes?"

Everything was gone. It was an empty journal. His findings. They were all gone. He flipped and found nothing. He got mad and tossed it.

"Great! Just fucking great!"

His computer turned on.

"Now what?" he said, rather annoyed.

Then the computer started typing on its own.

Borden, see you soon.

Borden, see you soon. Who wrote this?

That was all that was written.

"Is that it? More useless information. Who is going to see me soon?"

He couldn't journal anymore. There was no point, it seemed. He recalled everything that had happened to him thus far.

This wasn't a dream. I don't care how crazy that sounds, but that wasn't a dream. Whatever that was, I don't belong there. That's the second time I heard that. This means the graveyard wasn't a dream either.

His next thought might've broken his heart.

Olivia.

If none of those were dreams, did she eat the dirt off of the floor? What sick person would do that?

She's been lying to me. I don't even know who she is anymore, let alone where she is. Maybe she's not even at work!

She didn't even come home this time.

Borden spiraled out into the worst-case scenarios he could imagine.

I need to talk to her as soon as possible.

A door knob rattled.

Well, speak of the devil.

. . .

"Borden, honey, I'm home," Olivia called.

There was no worry in her voice and no sense of guilt for what she put Borden through by not coming home or calling him. This angered Borden. He wanted answers and met her at the entrance.

"Where were you, Olivia?"

Borden's foot tapped the floor, releasing the pent-up energy he struggled to control. He reminded himself to compose himself and slow down. "I've been worried about you!"

Olivia snubbed his aggressive attitude and responded, rather coldly.

"Work, ever heard of it?"

She made her way past him, contacting her shoulder.

"What is that supposed to mean?"

This is a rather rhetorical question from Borden. He didn't like what she was implying.

It was a low blow.

"It means what it means. Burden. I mean, Borden." she said, sporting a devilish grin as she untied her shoes.

"Fuck you, Olivia!"

"Oh, you don't like that? Poor big man needs his wife to take care of him. You want your Binky, Burden?"

The taunting continued, and Borden couldn't believe what he was witnessing.

"Who are you? This isn't you," he said.

"I'm going to bed. I have to work in the morning,"

"It **IS** the morning! You didn't come home all night,"

"Exactly, so I better get to sleep."

Door slam!

Her fading words cut Borden deep.

What just happened? Who was that? What was that?

There he stood in the living room, the ironic name of a room that felt so lifeless. He stood confused and powerless, with no strength left inside him to remove the dagger that had plunged into his heart.

7

THE BOAT MAN IS WAITING

A haunting whistle echoed through the locker room, fading away as the man wheeled his cart further down the hallway.

One afternoon, in the busy hospital cafeteria, a junior nurse sat enjoying her lunch break, which comprised a simple ham and cheese sandwich, most likely from the prepared refrigerated section. A paper crane was placed next to her plate on the table. Glancing up, she saw a young man with the goofiest grin on his face.

"Mind if I sit down?"

"I do," she said.

"Normally, you don't say that until we've gotten to know each other a little better," he said.

"In that case, I don't."

Continuing the conversation, he pointed at the paper crane on the table and asked, “What do you think?”

She said with a deadpan voice, “That’s cute. What is it? A dog?”

“It’s meant to wish someone good will and fortune.” He said, then asked, “Are you a nurse here?”

She pointed at her badge and said, “You must be in for a head injury.”

Despite her sarcastic tone, he enjoyed the banter.

“I’m actually here because of my heart. It’s not working very well, you see. I think it skipped a beat when I saw you.”

She rolled her eyes aggressively.

“Not a head injury, okay so, you’re just delusional then. Got it.”

“It’s a crane, a paper crane. And actually,” he said, fidgeting with it. “I know a great place around the corner. Would love to treat you to a drink.”

She took the last bite of her sandwich while he unfolded the crane in front of her, revealing a dollar.

She looked somewhat impressed at his magic trick.

“Oh yeah? Where is that?”

She called his bluff, leaning closer for dramatic effect.

“The vending machine. Around the corner. Want a Coke? Do you like coke?”

Her body language suggested that he won her over, sliding back into her chair with interest.

“That’s funny. I’ll give you that. No thanks. It’s at least a two-minute walk and I’m headed back into my shift.” She said, trading a playful but apologetic look.

“Well, that’s a good thing the Coke is already here.”

He revealed a can of Coke from his left hand. She shook her head, laughing into her chest.

"You walk around with Cokes in your pocket, offering them to girls sitting down in the cafeteria or what?"

"Sometimes," he said with a victorious smile.

"I liked the crane better," she said.

"Did you, now? Well, that's a shame, oh wait!" he said, turning over his hand and revealing a new paper crane. "It's actually right here!"

"Impressive, I'll admit. What's your name?"

"Borden."

"Nice to meet you, Borden. Thanks for the drink and the crane."

"And you are?"

"OLIVIA...OLIVIA!" a nurse called.

Olivia, staring at a can of Coke, snapped out of her flashback and said, "Yes? Sorry, I was, I was in my head."

Her coworker took a seat beside her.

"Yeah, I called you like thirty times. Everything okay?"

Olivia nodded in agreement, gesturing that she was perfectly fine. She fidgeted with the can of Coke and briefly mentioned the memory she was reminiscing about.

"This soda can. Borden once found me sitting for lunch and approached me with the most ridiculous amount of theatrics I had ever experienced. I liked it though. He was funny. He got me a Coke, out of his sleeve or something. Like magic."

A COUPLE of residents approached them.

"Come with us."

. . .

Olivia and the team of residents walked toward Daisy's room, gathering their things as they went. When they arrived, Olivia asked, "What seems to be the problem?"

The team explained that Daisy's EKG readings had been erratic for about five minutes, and despite being conscious, she had been screaming "Borden" repeatedly. They hoped that Olivia might have some insight into what was happening.

"Shortly after, she collapsed into the bed, and everything slowly returned to normal. I've never seen anything like this before," another resident said.

"We thought she might have been calling for you."

Intrigued, Olivia asked for some time alone in the room with Daisy. Once everyone left, she pulled over a rolling stool to sit by Daisy's bedside. After confirming that she was alone, she closed the door.

Daisy coughed and opened her eyes. Startled briefly, she chuckled and greeted Olivia.

"Hi sweetheart, I didn't hear you come in."

Olivia smiled back, the type of smile one gives at a wake.

"Daisy, are you feeling well?"

"Why yes, why do you ask?" Daisy said, her tired eyes barely visible, looking away towards the window.

Olivia struggled to approach her next line of questioning. She remembered the last encounter she had with Daisy and was curious to know if Daisy remembered any of it.

"I hear it, ya know. The knocking. At my window. Usually at night."

Olivia cleared her throat and asked, "What knocking?"

Daisy spoke slowly, so it took her a while to respond.

"The boatman. Yes, it's probably the boatman."

Closing her eyes and taking a deep breath, she released an immense sigh. Her lungs weren't as strong as they used to be, so she had to take a fast inhale afterward.

"Boatman?" Olivia asked.

No response.

Olivia patted her shoulder tenderly, calling her name, but Daisy was fast asleep.

The boatman? What is she talking about?

She attempted to wake her one more time but had no luck. Olivia stood up from her stool.

OVER THE SINK hung a dusty mirror, its edges stained with rust. Olivia caught her reflection as she rolled the stool towards the sink, but something seemed off. She blinked and looked again. There was someone there, behind her. But there couldn't be. She turned around, but the room was empty except for Daisy lying on the bed.

As Olivia sat beside her, the lights flickered in shades of red, casting eerie shadows on the walls. The room seemed to take on a life of its own. The air was so thick it was difficult to breathe.

"D-D-Daisy," she stuttered.

As Olivia took a measured step backward, her heart thumped against her ribcage, as if trying to escape its confines. She felt the frigid grasp of a pair of hands, like icy talons, curl around her shoulders. The chill that emanated from them was bone-deep and piercing, causing her entire body to shudder.

A gust of cold air, as sharp as a knife, rushed past her, inducing a wave of gooseflesh that erupted over her skin. With her eyes opened wide in terror and an overwhelming sense of dread that seemed to paralyze her overcame her mouth agape in a silent scream. It was as if an invisible force had seized her, tightening its grip with each passing moment, making it hard for her to even take a breath.

"Let him go." The breathy, low-pitched voice muttered behind her.

The acoustics of the room left the voice hanging in the air like a spectral being. A doorway violently carved itself into the barren wall, and this thing held Olivia's neck in place with an iron grip. She cried out in terror as the door creaked open, revealing a stampede of bodies pouring out in a chaotic frenzy.

The horde stumbled over each other, some falling at her feet while others clawed at her arms. They cut her screams short when a lifeless body seized her throat, rendering her silent. Her eyes bulged with fear, the whites showing through, as the room echoed with a chaotic chorus of animalistic growls and guttural snarls. the sound of the monitors beeping replaced the nightmarish din.

A group of nurses, residents, and hospital staff gathered around Olivia, who was convulsing and had foam at the corners of her mouth. They called out her name in a panicked voice, trying to figure out how to help her.

"Olivia!" a resident screamed, as they began administering chest compressions.

After a few moments, Olivia's eyes returned to their hazel color.

"Get off me! Get off me!" she squealed, her body writhing in complete panic as the residents tried to subdue her. Her arms flailed about as she cried hysterically, disoriented and confused.

"Please, give me a moment," Olivia said, her voice trembling.

She closed her eyes, trying to gather her thoughts and make sense of what had just happened. The memories flooded back to her. The knocking on the window, the stampede of bodies, the stiff hands on her shoulders. It had felt so real, so vivid. But it couldn't have been.

When she opened her eyes, she saw the concerned faces of her colleagues staring back at her. She took a deep breath and spoke. "I... I don't know what happened. I must have passed out or something."

The group of staff exchanged worried glances. One nurse stepped forward and put a hand on Olivia's shoulder.

She flinched.

"We should get you checked out, just to be safe."

Olivia dismissed the idea.

"I'm fine."

The residents traded looks with each other, realizing that what they had just witnessed was not a sign of someone fine. It was like something straight out of an exorcism documentary.

Showing great concern, Daisy reached out her hand and Olivia grabbed it.

"Are you okay, honey?"

"Yes, I'm fine."

She smiled and looked down at the table where she had placed Daisy's favorite vanilla pudding. She saw something strange—a paper boat.

Olivia, with curiosity, asked, "Where did you get that?"

Daisy, confused, looked over at the table and said, "Huh, would you look at that, a boat? No idea."

"Get some rest, Daisy," Olivia said, grabbing the boat.

. . .

In the locker room, Olivia sat at the center bench between the lockers, holding the paper boat in her hand. She was introspective and uneasy, fidgeting with the boat while examining it from different angles. She struggled to untangle her muddled and complex thoughts, like an intricate web.

A sense of fear pervaded her, a gnawing sensation in the pit of her stomach that refused to dissipate. The paper boat seemed like an enigma, a peculiar object she couldn't quite grasp or comprehend.

What does this mean? Was that the boatman in the room? The one that Daisy spoke of? Daisy said that she hears knocking every night. Something came over her the other day as well when she grabbed my arm and screamed at me. What did she say again? Something about letting go. Let him go, to be exact. Let who go?

The room went dark, causing Olivia to let out a scream. Abruptly, the lights returned.

An older man with a cart, one of its wheels squeaking, wheeled his way into the locker room.

"Sorry, my mistake. I hit the wrong switch here," he said. "Don't mind me, I'm just here to clean this place up a bit," he added with a laugh.

Still shaken from everything that had happened, Olivia's response came across as rude.

"Isn't it too early to clean, anyway?" realizing her bitter remark, she said, "Sorry, I just didn't expect anyone to show up, or rather, have the lights turned off on me."

"It was a mistake. What do you got there, sweetheart?" he called out, pointing at the paper boat in her hand.

The man wheeled his cart closer to her, hoarding some

knick-knacks at the bottom of the cart shelf. She noticed them and felt dismayed.

"Oh this, it's, I don't know."

"It looks like a boat," he said.

Olivia recognized she had been speaking in a confusing and unhelpful manner to someone who wasn't involved in her previous experiences. With that in mind, she changed the subject to something more pleasant.

"Yeah, you're right. It is a boat," she said, as she gave a soft chuckle. "It's one of those origami things I remember trying to make those. Could never get the creases right. I always wanted to make a crane."

That last word sank into her ear.

"A crane?"

The man nodded.

"My husband, he can make a crane," she said, looking down at the boat.

"Did he make that boat?"

The man noticed some tears swelling up in her eyes. Her response made it seem as if this was now a touchy subject.

"I'm sorry, trouble in paradise?" he asked.

"Not exactly, I don't know."

The man noticed Olivia's discomfort and tried to defuse the situation by offering some words of wisdom.

"You know, sometimes when you love someone, let them go," he said, with a glint in his eye that may have been from the overhead lights.

Olivia turned to him but remained silent.

The man's smile turned into a slow chuckle, which then morphed into a hideous laugh.

THE MAN STOPPED LAUGHING and said, "Well, I better get to cleaning. That's a nice boat. Have a good night."

A haunting whistle echoed through the locker room, fading away as the man wheeled his cart further down the hallway. She stowed the paper boat in her locker and shut it with a resounding clang. As she hurried towards the exit, she cast a wary glance over her shoulder. The whistle grew fainter and fainter until it vanished into the silence of the night.

Olivia approached the information desk with urgency.

"Hey Sarah, how's it going? Do you know who works in the sanitation department right now? An older guy, pretty tall."

Sarah took a moment to think before responding, "That's probably Emanuel, but he doesn't come in until 10:00 p.m. The only person on the sanitation shift right now is Evelyn, and she's not tall at all." She said, chuckling lightheartedly.

She forced a smile, revealing her dissatisfaction with the answer. She wondered who the man in the locker room was.

"Thanks, Sarah. Have a good night!" she said before turning and walking away.

SHE EXITED THE HOSPITAL, scanning the surroundings for anything or anyone suspicious. In the parking lot, she fumbled for her keys and dropped them by her car.

"Shit!" she grumbled.

As she reached down to retrieve them, a sound caught her attention: a dumpster lid closing. She looked up and saw the man from the locker room standing by the dumpster, illuminated by the light of a nearby street lamp. He made eye contact and waved his hand, but his smile looked sinister. Olivia ignored him.

The headlights of a passing car momentarily blinded Olivia as it pulled out of the hospital parking lot. Once the car was gone, she looked around, but the man she had seen earlier was nowhere to be found.

I'm losing my mind.

As Olivia drove to her mother's house, the whistling tune that echoed through the locker room corridors played over and over in her mind. She couldn't help but wonder about the old man and his cart, and what he had to do with the paper boat.

As she drove, she kept replaying the image of the man standing by the dumpster, giving her a sinister smile. She couldn't help but feel that something connected him to the strange occurrences that have been happening.

THE PAPER BOAT. It was such a small thing, yet it seemed to hold some sort of significance. Who made the paper boat and why did they leave it on Daisy's bedside table? She wondered.

I can't go home yet. Not like this.

8

MORE THAN JUST A PAPER CRANE

Her hand reached for her nightstand drawer and inside it was an ancient-looking paper crane.

A young man sat in a waiting room, visibly bored out of his mind. He got up and walked over to the receptionist.

"May I have a piece of paper?" he asked.

"Like a form? What do you need?" she asked.

The young man pointed to the printer and said, "No, just a simple white sheet of paper will do."

She rolled her chair over to the printer and rolled back. "Here you go."

He took the paper and thanked her, walking back to his chair. Slumped, he began creating the creases in the paper to fold it. A curious patient looked over at him. The young man made a cut by folding a sharp corner and then splitting it apart. The paper was now a perfect square.

The older gentleman sitting next to him leaned in and asked, "What are you making there?"

Without shifting his gaze away from the paper, he said, "A crane."

THE YOUNG MAN hesitated to speak to the older man because he had been spaced out and staring at everything as if he were lost. Maybe he was. After all, it was a hospital, the man could have dementia. The young man noticed the older man gazing with perplexed eyes, occasionally changing his expression.

"Trust the process," he said with a smirk.

A wing appeared, eliciting an excited laugh from the old man. Soon after, the head took its shape, and alas, a crane had been formed.

"Wonderful!" the old man called out, clapping his hands together.

He embraced the old man's cheer, waiting for the magic trick's last act, like a magician awaiting the prestige of his final act, and then lifted the crane into the air. One hand pinched the front part of the crane, whilst the other pinched the top of the tail end.

"Are you ready?" he asked.

Staring in eager anticipation, the older man nodded. The young man pulled on the tail end while holding the front stiff, causing the wings to flutter.

"Oh, my! That's amazing. How delightful," the older man said, his face painted with big rosy cheeks as he laughed himself into a wheezing cough.

"That's pretty cool, huh?" the young man remarked.

The older man looked at him and said, "You should give that to a special someone."

The young man shrugged, feeling flustered. "I saw a girl here, a nurse. Do you think she would like this?" he asked.

The older man looked at him intensely and said, "Listen, if I know anything about love and women, it's that they love to feel as if magic is real. They aren't naïve to it, but if you can make them feel, even for one second, that magic exists, you'll hold on to them for a very long time. Love by nature is modern-day magic, anyway. What else has the potential to make us do the crazy things that we do for it?"

As if he had just received the most intellectually simple advice he had ever heard, he agreed, laughing. "Yeah, I suppose you're right," the young man said. "What do they call you, sir? The love guru?" he sarcastically asked.

The man struggled to recall his own name.

"Something about you makes me feel at ease, sir. You have a very nice energy," the young man said.

"Thank you. You can call me Bob. How about you?"

"Borden."

A whisper in his ear interrupted a sleeping Borden.

He woke up alone in his bed. Olivia is nowhere in sight.

Why did I yell at her? I shouldn't have done that. I projected my own problems onto her. She wasn't wrong about getting her rest to work. It's the truth. I put myself in this position. I have to accept it for what it is.

He rolled over to face his nightstand. It had a picture in

a white frame of Olivia and Borden from their honeymoon. Borden squinted his eyes.

What is that?

He rubbed his eyes.

It's a crane.

A small paper crane, the same one he gave to Olivia years ago, sat on the nightstand next to a picture, and Borden felt tenderness in his chest.

"Oh Olivia, I feel as if I constantly disappoint you. I made you believe in magic, and now I'm showing you it doesn't exist," he said, pausing for a moment to collect his thoughts.

BORDEN JUMPED OUT OF BED, startled by the sound of books crashing onto the floor one by one. He watched as more books flew off the shelves, piling up on the ground. The headache that had plagued him before returned with a vengeance. He held his head in pain, trying to make sense of the chaos.

Amid it all, he noticed his laptop turning on and a Word document opening.

Why is my laptop in here? How did it get here?

The door swung back and forth, adding to the commotion. Borden struggled to decide where to focus his attention as the pain intensified.

He tried to read the text on the laptop screen with one eye open, but the sound of running water from the faucets and bathtub drowned out his attempts to comprehend what was happening.

The laptop read:

Borden, don't go, hold on

. . .

THIS WAS one of the worst headaches he had ever gotten. Everything had overwhelmed him; it was too much. He cried out for Olivia, chanting her name, wishing she would show up to soothe him.

"Olivia! Please! Help me! Everything hurts! Olivia!"

The screams were useless. There was no one home. Doors were swinging; the floor was flooding; books and other trinkets were flying off of the shelves; his head was about to explode; the laptop was communicating with him; he was overstimulated and Olivia was nowhere in sight.

MEANWHILE, back at the hospital, Olivia dealt with an emergency of her own. It was far worse. The condition of one of her patients from the critical care unit had exacerbated and triggered an alarm. Patient Room D was experiencing Olivia's worst-case scenario.

"No, no, what now? What is it now?"

Olivia rushed to the room, where a few interns and two other tenured doctors were huddled together in groups, discussing what the situation could be. Panting heavily, she arrived and asked for a status update.

They turned to her with solemn stares, and one of them spoke for all, "We don't know. We've never seen this before."

Olivia was distressed and scanned the room and the faces in it, seemingly hopeless and grasping at straws.

The other nurses and doctors present in the room noted the patient's condition was worsening with each passing second. Olivia was falling apart emotionally, and her professionalism had left her body.

One doctor said, "I think we know what we might have to do. I think this is a lost cause."

But Olivia screamed out, "No, no, no! We will not do that. Not yet! There is still time!"

The patient seized.

AT THE HOUSE, Borden was curled up against the wall of his bedroom, continuing to cry out for Olivia. He hyperventilated. His vision faded. Exhausted, he was ready to submit to whatever was coming. A silhouette appeared underneath the door frame. He couldn't concentrate on seeing who it was.

AT THE HOSPITAL, a nurse walked with a chart in her hand. Olivia took it aggressively from her hands.

She flipped the chart open, revealing a picture of the patient.

"Borden!" Stay with me!" Olivia cried, tears streaming onto the chart.

A lifeless Borden convulsed in front of a group of medical professionals and his own wife, Olivia, who desperately tried her hardest to keep him alive. Suddenly, the vitals returned to a healthy state, and Borden returned to his coma.

"**Patient D: Angier Borden, seems to be stable now**."

Olivia sobbed into her husband's body on the bed. She squeezed his hand and pleaded with his unconscious body.

"You can't leave me yet, Borden, please. I can help you. I love you."

An ominous presence entered Borden's bedroom at the house.

"Olivia," he called out.

The shadowy silhouette cleared up and everything around settled.

"Hi honey, it's me. You're okay now," Olivia said as she approached him.

Borden, unsure if he was awake or dreaming, and evidently unaware of this false reality, said, "You have to believe me. Everything was moving. There is something wrong in this house." He said with frustration, "I'm sorry for the other day. I didn't mean to yell at you."

Olivia pulled his head into her chest, reassuring him that everything was okay. But as she looked over at the computer, a sinister smile formed on her face. A bitter and twisted look struck her features, and her eyes glinted with dark malice. She didn't appreciate what the computer was transmitting, but instead of feeling worried or concerned, she looked pleased by the information.

I thought you were finally gonna leave me, Borden. I'm scared. What should I do? Do you want me to let you go? Are you suffering? Please wake up Borden. Wake up.

Olivia stood inside Patient Room D, staring at her husband, Borden, who lay motionless in his ongoing coma.

She leaned in closer and whispered to him, hoping her words could penetrate his unconscious mind.

THE LAPTOP at the house continued,

> Borden, Hold on!

Whoever this Olivia was, she was not happy with the words relayed on the computer screen. Her mild amusement from before had vanished.

She continued to read:

> Please, wake up Borden! Wake up!

Olivia looked at Borden, noticing that he had blacked out. She brought her menacing stare back up towards the laptop. With a single look, the laptop snapped shut and got launched at the wall, shattering into pieces.

"We don't need any outside advice now, do we?" she said to Borden.

Wherever Borden was, the laptop was relaying a message of whatever was being heard in Patient Room D. There was a connection between both realms. But that was gone now. She had made sure of it.

"Don't worry Borden, you're okay," she said in a soothing voice, rocking back and forth. "It is almost time, soon we'll be on our way." Borden, resting in Olivia's arms, slept peacefully on the floor of his perceived office.

A NURSE APPROACHED the real Olivia at the hospital.

"Are you okay?" the nurse asked.

Emotionally and physically exhausted, Olivia said curtly, "No, I'm not."

There was a long pause between them, and neither knew what to say.

"Listen, I can't imagine what you're going through, but..." The nurse trailed off, unsure of how to continue.

Olivia turned to her with a pained expression. "No, you can't. You don't understand. I can't sleep, and sometimes I can't even think. I hear things, I see things. Things that shouldn't exist, let alone, talk to me."

THERE WAS anger in Olivia's voice as she continued. "Sometimes I feel like Borden is trying to communicate with me. It sounds crazy, but I just feel like he's asking me to let him go. That I should just let them pull the plug. Another part of me feels like he's calling my name like he's trapped somewhere and needs my help to get out."

Olivia took a deep breath. Her friend, listening profoundly, shook off a feeling of uneasiness. Olivia continued.

"Daisy mentioned the boatman. I don't know what that is, but she said that the boatman was waiting for her. I think I saw the boatman. Is he here for Borden? This sounds insane. Am I just grasping at straws here? What if I'm being tricked into letting him go, making it easier for the boatman to take him?" Olivia asked, her voice trembling.

Her friend struggled to find the right response and finally suggested, "Maybe you're the reason he's still here in the first place? I don't know about any of those things, nor do I believe in that stuff, but I think if he's still here, it's for a reason. I don't think you should give up hope."

Olivia wiped the tears from her eyes and looked over at her friend. She thanked her for her genuine support.

"Olivia, go home, I insist. Go home and get some rest. You've been here for hours," the nurse said with concern.

Reluctantly, Olivia accepted the offer. She had been determined to stay by Borden's side at all times. But as his recent emergencies became more and more clear, she became too emotionally attached to aid the other patients effectively.

LEANING OVER TO BORDEN, Olivia placed one hand on her chest and the other on his. Tears filled her eyes as she whispered, "Borden, I hope you can hear me."

THE SHATTERED fragments of the computer screen began to glitch and flicker back to life, powered by something far beyond its physical realm. Soon, a message appeared on the damaged screen.

> I will never give up on you. Borden. I want you to know that—

OLIVIA KISSED his forehead and finished her last words. "—I love you."

Olivia said her last goodbyes and left Borden's side. She stood in the doorway and took one final look back. There he lay, motionless, yet peaceful. Olivia wished he would show any signs of life, but she knew it was unlikely. She blew him a kiss and walked away.

THE RIDE HOME WAS QUIET, but the sounds in her head were loud enough to drown out any noise. Olivia hadn't been home in a while, always going to her mother's house instead because the thought of being in their home without Borden was too painful.

AS OLIVIA ENTERED the dark and empty house, the creaking of the old wooden floors under her feet made her feel like she was walking through a deserted house that had been abandoned for years. The dust-covered windows and the wild overgrown grass outside were a stark contrast to the once-beautiful and lively home she had known. The memories of her and Borden's time together flooded her mind, making her heart heavy with sadness.

She moped toward the table by the entryway, feeling every inch of the house's emptiness. As she placed her keys down, the sound echoed through the stillness of the house. She stood still for a moment, trying to gather her thoughts and emotions.

With a deep breath, she flicked the light switch, illuminating the dimly lit room. The sudden brightness caused her to squint her eyes, but as they adjusted, she noticed the dusty furniture and the cobweb-filled corners of the room. Olivia couldn't help but feel like the heart and soul of the house had disappeared, along with Borden.

She walked through the lifeless rooms, feeling more and more isolated as she went. She walked into her bedroom and sat on the edge of her bed. Her hand reached for her nightstand drawer and inside it was an ancient-looking paper crane. She pulled it out and held it in her hands, tracing the edges of the crane with her fingers, and then placed it on her nightstand to stare at. It reminded her of the day Borden gave it to her. The memories of the happy times they had shared now seemed like a distant dream.

The moment she walked into the kitchen, she hit the lights and pulled out the chair that she used to sit across from Borden. It was the spot where they had their funny conversations or heated debates about trivial things. She sat down and stared at the space before her, wishing for Borden's presence to be there.

UNBEKNOWNST TO HER, Borden was also in the kitchen, sitting in his correct seat across from her. Lost in thought, Borden was reflecting on his situation. The two of them sat at the dining table, like two lost souls existing in parallel universes, sharing the same physical space but separated by different realms.

OLIVIA STARED at the empty chair before her.

Oh, Borden, I wish you were here.

BORDEN'S NECK hair stood up, and a tenderness swelled in his chest, giving him a feeling of hope. As Olivia's thoughts seemed to pierce through the invisible veil separating them, suddenly, he sensed a presence in front of him, and his eyes moved towards the empty chair, where Olivia should have been seated.

Olivia? He thought.

Olivia, I swear I won't yell at you ever again. I love you with every fiber of my being. I will never give up on us. You believe magic is real because of my silly paper tricks. I believe magic is real because you exist.

AT THAT MOMENT, Borden's boundless thoughts had traversed the realm of possibility, and just like that, Olivia felt a breeze in the air, her skin turning to goosebumps. She sensed Borden's presence as if he was sitting in front of her, playing one of his silly tricks and laughing in his obnoxious way.

She wasn't afraid, for the sensation was one of pure love. At that moment, it was as if their thoughts had transcended the boundaries of space and time, their love serving as an ethereal conduit between two separate worlds. Though separated by dimensions, they remained connected by an unbreakable bond that surpassed all understanding.

For in the realm of love, the distance was a mere illusion, and their souls were forever intertwined.

9
THE GREAT PRETENDER

I want her to look down at this watch and think of me and how we have all the time in the world now that we've tied the hands of time.

For the first time in a long while, the house was filled with peace and tranquility. A softly glowing candle illuminated their cozy kitchen, casting a loving and intimate ambiance over the table where Borden and Olivia sat. It was as if they were on a romantic date, enjoying each other's company in a way that only inseparable lovebirds could.

In the living room, their favorite hits were blasting through the speakers, adding to the atmosphere of love and relaxation. The soothing crackle of the fireplace completed the picture of an ideal evening, a much-needed respite for Borden after a long and trying period.

"I love that sound," Borden said, taking a bite of his pizza.

"What sound?" Olivia asked.

"The fire, the way it crackles."

"Oh, yes. It is nice. I agree."

"Fun fact, there are studies that prove the sound of a crackling fire can reduce blood pressure," Borden said with a convincing smile.

"Is that so?"

"Yeah, try it on your patients," he said, laughing.

"Next time I have a patient with hypotension, I'll put them next to a fire," she said sarcastically.

THE TWO OF THEM LAUGHED, the banter reminiscent of the day they met. Cheeks crimson with joy, the laughter slowly settled. Borden wiped his mouth with a napkin and cleared his throat.

"You mean hypertension," Borden said, correcting her as he took another bite.

"What did I say?" Olivia asked.

"Hypotension," he said with a mouth full of cheese and pepperoni.

"Right, that's what I meant. Hypertension," she said.

"Hypertension is a sign of high blood pressure, with hypotension meaning the opposite," Borden mused, finding it strange for Olivia to make such a simple mistake.

"Hypo, hyper, it's so easy to mix up. I see it so often, ya know." She said, redeeming herself in his eyes.

"Yeah, of course. I get it," he said, as he brought another slice of pizza onto his plate.

The evening continued.

"I missed this," Borden said, gesturing to himself and Olivia. "Us, like this. Something simple, pizza, and a decent laugh. A good time. I missed this."

"I missed it too. I've spent so much time at the hospital lately, I almost forgot how nice it is." She said, smiling back.

Borden had a rapid idea, a lightbulb moment. He thought it would be cute.

"Maybe I can come down to the hospital one day. We can sit in the cafeteria. I'll get you a Coke," he said, feeling a sense of shyness creeping up on him.

"No, I don't think so. It's a nice thought, but I don't think so," she said, and Borden's heart sank. Suddenly, the pizza tasted sour, and his appetite vanished.

"Well, why not? Don't you have a lunch break?" he asked, trying to keep his tone stern.

"No. There's no time for breaks. Why don't we focus on enjoying our dinner, Borden?" Olivia asked,

"No time for breaks? That's your excuse? It wouldn't take longer than five minutes. You're telling me you wouldn't have five minutes at all to spare from your thirty-seven-hour shift?" Borden asked.

"I didn't work thirty-"

Borden **slammed** his hand on the table.

"That's not the point. I was exaggerating, but that's not the point."

Olivia's demeanor changed.

Borden stared at her with a probing gaze, looking at Olivia as if she were a witness he was cross-examining. Except, he kind of was. Olivia felt this and didn't like it. She became defensive.

"What is this really about, Borden?" She said, placing her hands on the table.

"You know what this was about."

"Vague. Real vague there."

"You're acting strange, Olivia. You have been coming home late, and just the other night, you didn't even come home."

"I was busy. At work. As you should be, but you're home and moping, crying, and complaining. Whining like a little bitch all the damn time!" Olivia screamed, getting louder, gesturing with her hands, amplifying the magnitude of her words.

"I slave away, and meanwhile all you do is 'me, me, me, me. My head hurts. I see monsters,' you know how asinine that sounds. Do you know how infuriating it is to come home to that? Gods, sometimes I wish I could just speed up this entire process and end it!"

"End it. End what?" Borden asked, his voice breaking.

"Never-mind. It's nothing."

"No, tell me, Olivia. What?"

Reluctant to speak, Olivia got up from the table. Borden's voice and eyes followed her.

"See, this is what I'm talking about. You shut down. You say these outlandish and hurtful things to me. Then you just leave? This isn't you. Where were you the other night? Why didn't you reach out to me? Why have you been lying to me, about the chairs, about understanding me? Why did you lie about the dirt from that night on the kitchen floor? You didn't cause that, Olivia!" Borden shouted, crying out his frustration at Olivia as he followed her into the living room.

Olivia was looking for ways to respond, but Borden overwhelmed her with a bombardment of accusations.

"Why do we have the wrong cereal? Why are you so nonchalant about the things I tell you that occur to me?"

"Because you're crazy. They don't exist. You're fabricating them. You bring them into existence, Borden!" She called out.

"What happened to my journal?"

"Why should I know?"

"It's empty! Everything I wrote, gone!"

"That's not my problem!" She screamed.

"There's someone else, isn't there?" Borden said, getting quiet.

"What makes you say that?"

"You don't wear the watch I gave you anymore. You don't come home. You work countless amounts of overtime. You're forgetting the little things that make us work." Borden said.

"I don't wear it while I'm working because I don't want it to get contaminated with bodily fluids. I have it, though. Here, it's in my pocket." Olivia said, pulling out a watch from her pocket.

She threw the watch at Borden. He caught it and gripped it close to his face. He studied it. Exhausted from the conversation, he noticed something, nevertheless, he stopped antagonizing her.

"Olivia, I'm.."

"Yeah, fuck you, Borden," she said, walking past him, brushing against his shoulder.

He turned to look at her as she grabbed a coat and headed for the door.

"Where are you going?" He asked.

"Out!"

"Where,"—

The door slammed.

. . .

THE CRACKLING fire and ambient music still played in the background, depicting an irony to Borden's feelings. He collapsed onto the couch.

This watch. This watch is not the one I gave her.

He had no more tears left for her, his soul crushed, and his suspicions now accepted as true.

The engraving. It's not here. This watch is a terrible imitation. A fake. Why would she have a fake version of the watch I gave her? I'd understand if she lost it and secretly got a new one to replace it. I'd believe that for a second. Until the moment she can confidently give it to me and expect me to believe it's the real one, knowing damn well, without the engraving, it would be a dead giveaway that it wasn't the real one.

BORDEN ALWAYS KNEW that Olivia never wore her watch at work, and there was a reason for it. As he sat with the fake watch in his hand, memories flooded back to Olivia's 25th birthday.

THEY HAD BEEN DATING for a couple of years, and Olivia was still working as a nurse, while Borden was a printer sales associate, among other computer accessories.

On that special day, Borden had prepared a bouquet of roses and a small wooden box for Olivia, which he had kept in the trunk of his car. As he arrived at Mariana's house, he carefully retrieved the gifts and approached the door with a proud smile on his face.

He held the sun-kissed roses delicately behind his back

as he knocked. Three consecutive knocks, followed by a pause, and then two more knocks. That was his usual knock pattern. A younger Mariana, with no gray hair yet, opened the door with a delightful smile, and they embraced.

"Is she here yet?" Borden asked eagerly.

"No, she's almost off work, though. You came at a good time," she said, guiding him into the house.

"Anything I can help set up?"

"Yes actually. Do you mind putting up the streamers and balloons? It's hard for me to reach up there."

"Of course, no problem!"

After having everything ready to go for Olivia's surprise party, the two of them shared a moment of conversation. Curious to know what was inside the box, she asked Borden what he had got her.

"A watch. Nothing special," he said.

"Nonsense, I'm sure it's very special."

"Well, it's got this engraving on it. I think she'll like it," Borden said, flipping the watch over, revealing the sentimental detail.

"Oh Borden, it's wonderful. She's going to love it. Maybe now she can be on time for a change." She said.

They both laughed.

"It's funny that you mention that because—"

Back home on the couch, Borden returned from his memory and quoted his past self, "—it doesn't work. It isn't meant to work. Whenever she feels that time is fleeting, I want her to look down at this watch and think of me and how we have all the time in the world now that we've tied the hands of time."

The hands of time, huh? What a load of shit.

Borden's thumb caressed the spot without the engraving. Engraving or not, the fact that it worked had already let him know it wasn't the one he gave her. The watch never worked. Olivia knew this. He threw the watch carelessly and took a deep breath.

What's going on? Who is this person? This isn't Olivia. Not the Olivia that I know. She's not Olivia-

That's when it hit him.

"She's not," he said, jumping out of the chair and taking an athlete's stance. "She's not. That's what the nurse said. She's not."

BORDEN'S MIND wandered through various thought labyrinths as he tried to piece together the puzzle.

What was it? I can't remember. The fucking journal. I sure could use that right now. The nurse from the kitchen pointed towards her and was saying something about, 'She's not' but never finished the sentence. Olivia is so against my dreams or visions, or whatever they are! Why? They always come with some form of warning. That's not a bad thing. That's a good thing. But if that's the good thing, then what's the bad thing?

The connections made more sense.

Why did she lie about the dirt? The dirt was evidence of my delusions. Or, a reality that she's preventing me from believing to be real? The journal, too, was evidence of my delusions. Now that's gone as well?

His neurons fired up at the revelations in his head.

If I'm wrong about this, it won't be good for my psyche

because this is some far-fetched stuff I'm going towards. Everything feels wrong. I wake up, shit happens, I see Olivia, I sleep, and repeat. All she mentions is that trip. What trip? Where are we going? Why doesn't she tell me? We have the wrong cereal in the house. She sits in the wrong places and calls me the wrong name.

It feels as if Olivia's been kidnapped and replaced by some clone that's just pretending to be her. This is the premise of a stupid sci-fi movie. My dreams all warn me about staying away or being somewhere I don't belong. Where is that place exactly? Where shouldn't I be? Is it this place? My home? Is this even my home? The hallway walls were mirrored, and the floor was coming off like some sort of wallpaper until it magically sealed up.

Is the house pretending to be my house? Who's responsible for this? Am I just that delusional?

Borden seemed to be on the precipice of discovery when the subject in question made their return.

"Olivia, Hi!"

A flustered Borden suspiciously greeted Olivia as she walked back in. She noticed something was off.

"Hello? I forgot something." She said, glancing back at him with curiosity.

"Yeah, ok. Sure. Listen, I'm sorry for what I said. For ruining our night."

Olivia remained silent.

"I hope we can move forward. I don't want to waste time arguing over such trivial things."

"Trivial?" She asked. "Trivial? Borden, those were accusations. Of a high degree!" She shouted.

"Yes, yes. You're right. I'm sorry. Truly."

Borden appeared remorseful and willing to reconcile with her.

"I still have to go out."

"That's fine. Whatever you need. I'm here for you. If you, ya know, need anything." Borden fumbled around with his speech. He appeared strangely suspicious.

"Okay, thanks, Borden. I appreciate that." She said, dry as ever.

Borden had an unusual smile on his face. It appeared he was the one doing the pretending now.

Olivia left once again.

BORDEN LET OUT a deep sigh as if it had averted a crisis. The train of thoughts he was derailing from forced him to rethink the matter at hand.

Okay, okay. If I'm on to something here, I have to be careful. For now, I just have to be mindful of what I say and do. From this point on, I'll be the agreeable and healthy Borden. No problems, just love for my wife. I need to buy more time and find out what's really going on. I can do that. I can definitely play along.

Borden the burden, no. Borden, the great pretender.

10

MISE EN SCÈNE

Yeah, we're definitely inside of a movie, Borden. Someone wanted to make a movie about two morons in love

---

Cotton candy skies and the setting sun provided entertainment for Borden as he sat on his porch, taking in the outdoors. A gentle breeze rocked his chair, creating a tranquil scene that anyone else could have enjoyed forever.

But not Borden.

His gaze was fixed on the horizon as he rocked back and forth. Although the chirping of birds caught his attention for a few seconds, he couldn't help but analyze their sounds. The chirps were beautiful, but his recent paranoia made him question their very existence.

I've been staring at this sun for 37 minutes. It hasn't moved an inch.

On his lap was the same journal he had used before, with his pen at the ready to jot down any new pieces of information he noticed.

That bird. Every 4 minutes it chirps the exact same thing. The rhythm, the volume, everything. The same. Repeated. Interesting.

Despite his findings, he remained incredibly calm. He wasn't overstimulated, and his headaches weren't bothering him. He couldn't help but feel at peace, regardless of his intentions. He felt liberated to a certain extent.

There!

Borden sat up and stopped the rocking of his chair, leaning forward and pressing down on the armrests. He squinted his eyes as a placebo to view longer distances and scribbled down more bits of information.

Borden raised his hand in the air.

"Five, four, three, two, one," he said, snapping his finger and pointing towards a tree.

Chirp! Chirp!

"There it is!" he shouted, like a madman or a mad scientist gleaming with maniacal joy at the success of his lab experiment. He wrote down more data in his journal.

"This is wild." He said, nodding his head. "Is this one giant pile of shit or what? Where are the cameras?"

His sense of humor overshadowed his desperation, serving as a coping mechanism. It sounded like a joke, but in reality, he was scared about what he was noticing and what it might mean for him if he was right about it all.

"What's wild?" Olivia asked, standing in the doorway stirring a tea of some kind.

Borden closed his journal and smiled at her.

"That view. Isn't it breathtaking? That's a view to kill for, wouldn't you agree?"

"That's a strange thing to say, but I suppose you're right." Olivia replied.

She walked over to him and leaned on the hand rail.

"Writing again huh?"

"Yeah, I figured I would start a diary. Talk about my day and the things I'm grateful for."

"Am I in there?" she asked, smirking.

"I'm thinking about putting you in there, but it's only got so many pages, and I don't know if I'll have the space—"

Borden started to laugh before he could finish his sentence.

"—Oh please. Spare me. I wish to be in your little 'what I'm grateful for' diary." she pleaded sarcastically.

"Well, since you asked so kindly." he joked.

Olivia stirs her tea.

"I made this for you."

"Oh that's sweet. I already had mine though. Sorry!" he said, revealing a mug down on the floor.

Olivia seemed displeased. She fidgeted with the mug in her hand, not knowing what to do with it.

"Why don't you drink it honey?" Borden suggested.

"I'm not thirsty, I made it for you."

"Yeah well, we've covered that part." he shrugged. "Again, I'm sorry, but it was very thoughtful of you."

Olivia's body language became inquisitive. Borden noticed, adjusting his own body to counter hers.

Am I being too obvious here? I am, aren't I? I'm never been overly thankful. Shit, she must have noticed something's off. She's reading me. I have to think of something.

"Borden, is everything okay?"

"Yeah! Why wouldn't it be? I'm with you, my loving wife. Whom I care for very deeply. And wish to spend my entire life with." He replied, laughing nervously.

Real smooth moron. Real smooth.

OLIVIA SEEMED confused at the way Borden was responding to her. Considering the argument they recently had, it was strange for Borden to be so elated.

"You sure you're okay, Borden? How are your headaches."

"Gone! Haven't had any. It's the strangest thing."

"That's good news. You seem much happier."

"I am. Life is good. Look at that view." Borden said, gesturing out to the horizon.

Olivia took a look, humoring him.

Maybe I shouldn't.

A look appeared in Borden's eye. An idea.

Screw it.

"Hey Olivia. Does anything look strange to you?" Borden asked.

"Strange? How so?"

"Ya know, strange. Anything out of the ordinary?"

"It's nature. Everything is out of the ordinary."

Borden laughed, admiring that insightful response. "That's good. Clever. Absolutely right." He replied. "But even so, some things have a natural consistency to them. I mean, the Earth rotates so many days a year, or the sun for example. It goes down every night, and comes up every morning. Some things aren't so out of the ordinary."

The two of them have entered an unsolicited game of chess, a mind game. As if both of them were concealing their true intentions and speaking metaphorically in order to address the elephant in the room.

"Well Borden, that's what nature is. They say that lightning never strikes twice, and yet, we've seen lightning strike the same spot more than ten times." She said.

"That's fair. Some things just can't be explained I suppose. The universe around us is therefore a misunderstood beauty." Borden replied.

"Precisely." Olivia stated, winning her case.

Olivia took that moment as an opportunity to walk back into the house. She seemed pleased with herself, but not so much at Borden for striking up a conversation about the world around them. Borden noticed her becoming uncomfortable by speaking about this.

Let's fly a bit closer to the sun, shall we?

Borden grabbed her hand as she was walking past him, holding her steady.

"It's hard, I should say, to argue against the scientific certainties of the universe." Borden stated, opening the door to the conversation once more. "I think it's fair to agree that some things should remain consistent, wouldn't you say?"

Olivia's smile, painted in a churlish manner. She pulled her hand out of his grasp. Gently.

"What do you mean, Borden?" Olivia remarked, visibly agitated.

Think about this for a second. We don't know how she'll react.

Borden hesitated.

Olivia, waited for a reply, with eyes that appeared soulless.

Borden went for it, pushing the boundaries of her comfort zone.

"You see that sun?"

"Yeah," she replied.

"That sun has been in the same spot for the last hour."

"What do you mean?"

"I mean, that sun should've been way below the horizon by now."

"So what are you insinuating?"

"Nothing. You don't find that odd?" Borden replied, combatting her defensive stance.

"Yeah, I guess. Who cares?"

"Want to see a magic trick?"

"What?"

"Magic. Want to see a magic trick?"

Olivia began to tremble, stuttering in her replies. Borden pushed it further. His goal was to overstimulate her with these outlandish details of a strange world. There must be a reason as to why she didn't appear comfortable talking about this.

"Yeah, sure. Why not."

"Great. Okay, so indulge me for a second."

"What do you mean?"

"Nothing, just wait, give me a minute here." Borden said, looking down at his watch.

Olivia fidgeted at her clothing. Borden decided to antagonize her a bit more while they waited.

"You okay there?"

"Yeah, I'm fine. What are we waiting for exactly?" she asked.

"Hold on, almost time."

"Borden, I have things–"

Borden interrupted her, swinging his hand over yonder.

"—three, two, one. There!"

Chirp! Chirp!

Borden laughed and clapped ecstatically. Olivia didn't share the same enthusiasm. She looked annoyed, even.

"Isn't that cool? Like magic, you like magic right?" Borden poked at her.

"Yeah, I do."

"The bird. It chirped right on schedule."

"What do you mean on schedule?" she asked with confusion.

"Well, since you believe that some things are just out of the ordinary, I thought you would like to see me predict the bird's chirp," Borden said, swallowing his nervousness.

"Predict? How is that a thing?"

"Olivia, precisely every 4 minutes, the same chirp! On the dot!"

"Okay? What does that mean?"

"That's not weird to you at all?"

"Birds chirp. It's just a coincidence. Probably a different bird." she said, dismissing his claims.

"Not this, no. It's the same bird, in the same tree." Borden confidently stated. "That's not the only weird thing. There's many other weird things that don't make sense. It feels like we're on the production of a movie set."

Borden laughed, only to prove to Olivia that he's not suspicious of her. Deep down, he's dead serious.

"Yeah, we're definitely inside of a movie, Borden. Someone wanted to make a movie about two morons in love," she joked, returning back to a higher level of comfort.

"I don't know, I'm just goofing around." Borden stated, laughing at the crazy ideas he brought up.

OLIVIA TOOK A BREATH OF RELIEF. Her body, once tense, now soft and limber as ever. She approached Borden, sitting on his lap.

"You're a strange man yourself."

"Yes, yes I am."

"Hey Olivia," he said.

"Yeah?"

"Why aren't you at work today?" Borden asked, as Olivia stood up offended at the comment. Borden continued, "don't get me wrong, I enjoy having you here, but I thought you'd be at work today."

Olivia stood distant. She looked away towards the horizon and back to Borden.

"I took the day off."

"The day off?"

Borden was surprised. "The day off? You? In what world do you ever take a day off?"

"I took a few days off actually." she responded with a smile.

"Whoa wait a minute. Who are you and what have you done with Olivia?" he joked.

"We have to get ready for our trip. It's taking a little longer than I expected, so we'll have to wait a bit. I figured we might as well spend some time together getting ready for it."

"That's unheard of. I can't complain about that though." Borden said.

Borden took a moment. He finally found the courage to ask.

"Where are we going anyway?"

"I don't want to spoil the surprise."

"By all means, spoil it." Borden suggested.

"No," she replied.

"Come on, where, what is it?"

Olivia, flustered, she caved in.

"A cruise."

"A cruise?"

"Yeah! I think it will be fun." she said.

"Like a boat?" Borden asked, not because he was unsure, but because he was afraid of the answer.

"Well, yeah. Just, a big boat I guess." Olivia replied.

"Sounds fun," Borden remarked.

"You sure, cause you look like you've seen a ghost."

Borden's mind circled his puzzle pieces while he tried to maintain a composed demeanor.

"It'll be great. Thanks. Do you mind if I stay out here a bit longer? I'll be inside in a moment or two."

"Knock yourself out. Dinner in 30 minutes. Don't be late." she said, smiling as she entered the house.

Borden smiled back.

A cruise. A boat. Boat. Boat. Boat. I was pulled away from a boat. That thing seemed to warn me about the boat. Should I be worried? Just what is this boat? I can't go on this cruise. I need more answers. She clearly didn't enjoy that conversation whatsoever. Anytime I alluded to the fact that this was all one giant facade, her blood pressure dropped. If I am in a facade, how did I get here?

Let's be rational about this. The answers, no matter how irrational, I must be rational about it. Why am I in this facade? Why would she be in on it? Tricking me into believing this is real?

None of this is real. That sun doesn't move. The animals are looped. The trees are copy and pasted. I'm on a movie set, but who is filming? Who's movie is this?

BORDEN'S THOUGHTS came to a close, perfectly timed.

"Three,"
"Two,"
"One,"
Chirp! Chirp!

11

ALL ALONG THE WATCHTOWER

"That's a good song," she said, moments before dissipating into thin air.

The glares of a morning sunrise brighten the skies and pierced through the trees as animals exited their burrows, skittish and loud, eager to start their day. Olivia was serenaded by the sounds of nature, holding a cup of tea in her hand and rocking gently back and forth on her porch chair while witnessing the wonders of the Earth.

I wish you were here, Borden.

The chirping of the birds gathered on a branch brought both joy and sorrow to her. Their display of affection brought forth a sense of longing, for she too wanted what the birds had - to brush up against the person she loved, to eat with them, to play with them, and everything in between.

Her sleep was fitful. It felt strange being in the house altogether. Olivia stepped out in the middle of the night at one point. She had been awake since, a witness to the nightlife. She watched as the full moon worked the night shift and clocked out, making way for the day shift crew. Then, the majestic sun rose and exercised its dominion over all beneath it.

Life moves on. Maybe I should too. Maybe Borden needs to. Except he can't do it on his own. He needs me to do it for him. Is it wrong for me to extend his suffering with nothing but hope for him to wake up again? Am I being selfish?

THE BEAUTY of life in front of her, the panoramic views, made her wonder about what life would be like if she let Borden go.

The wind, the warmth of the sun–this could be Borden's energy that I embrace. Every ray of light that kisses my face could be Borden. When it rains, it would be as if Borden was weeping for me. Any disaster would be Borden letting me know it's time to join him.

Instead, these views, these moments, are hollow. How can I appreciate this, knowing that I can't share this with the one I love? Knowing he's in a dark room, tied to machines that allow him to exist. Tied to machines that help him breathe. His physical body is tied to this world. Why do I have to be the one to decide? It just doesn't seem fair. It's not fair to me. It's not fair to him. I'm not ready to decide whether he dies, or continues to be half-dead with only the hope that he lives.

. . .

Olivia's reflection was cut short when she heard something coming from inside the house. The radio. It was playing a song in the living room.

She entered cautiously, staying near the doorway as she scanned the room.

"Hello?" she asked timidly. "My husband is going to be home in a minute, so if there's anyone here, please leave." She said, trying to sound intimidating.

No response.

The music continued to play. A tune by the great Jimi Hendrix.

All Along the Watchtower? Borden loves that song.

"He has a gun!" she shouted.

Still no answer.

She trudged to the radio, tiptoeing to be as subtle as possible.

Click!

She turned it off. The house remained quiet. Occasional creaks, but she was sharp enough to recognize them as being casual house sounds.

A small gasp escaped her when the song played again.

Click!

Not a second after shutting off, when the song started itself again.

Afraid now, she unplugged the radio from the outlet. She felt foolish staring at a radio that was unplugged, expecting it to work. For once, a moment of normalcy, it did not play again.

"That was weird." She said aloud.

"What was weird?" a voice asked.

"What the hell, Mom?" Olivia screamed at the top of her lungs. Her soul had seemingly left her body.

. . .

"Sorry, didn't mean to scare you like that," Mariana apologized, with a snicker at the end. Mariana won't ever miss an opportunity to tease her.

"I swear, you and Borden, no wonder you two get along."

"What? It's funny." Mariana shrugged.

"What are you doing here, anyway?"

"You didn't come over last night, so I was worried about you."

"I should've mentioned it, but I forgot," Olivia said, becoming emotional.

This wasn't a time for Mariana to tease her.

"What's wrong, honey?"

Olivia replied, in a breaking voice, "B-Borden, he, he almost died yesterday."

"So he's okay now?"

"Well, I think so. We stabilized him and he returned to a coma." She cried. "But it was so close this time. I thought I lost him."

"The good news is that he's okay for now," Mariana suggested.

"Last night when I got here, I sat at the table, and I could've sworn I felt Borden's presence. I felt him sitting there with me. Part of me was expecting a phone call, letting me know that he didn't make the night." She said, looking down at her watch.

Mariana noticed her distress and made an attempt to offer some words of encouragement.

"Maybe he was here, Olivia, in spirit. His body is at the hospital, but you carry him with you," she said, placing her hand on Olivia's heart. "He lives there, always, in death or in life. He will always be there, in that big ol' heart of yours."

Olivia responded well to Mariana's wisdom. She cried and laughed at how much sense her mom seemed to make.

"You're right. It just hurts."

"Well, that's part of the deal. You get to carry him around, but a toll must be paid. With love comes sadness. And madness," she joked. "Even when he does something stupid, you'll feel it."

Olivia smiled.

"So what was weird?" Mariana asked.

"Oh, umm. The radio, it turned itself on."

"Brujeria!" Mariana said. "Witchcraft. No, no, don't tell me those things. I don't like them."

"I know! Me too, Mom, you know that. But I can't pretend like it didn't happen." She replied.

"Well, what happened exactly?" Mariana asked.

"I was outside and then I heard the radio turn on. I thought someone was inside, so I was scared to enter. When I did, the house was empty, but the music was playing. It was one of Borden's favorite songs."

"There it is!"

Mariana interrupted her, placing her hand on Olivia's heart once more, proving her past point. "That was Borden, sweetie."

"You think so?" a vulnerable Olivia replied.

"It had to be. You're in this house, a house filled with love. You carry Borden around. His energy slipped out and put on his tunes. He's trying to communicate with you." She said with confidence in her voice.

"It's interesting that you say that."

"What do you mean? There's more?"

"Well, lately. There're moments where I feel as if he's

talking to me. Instilling thoughts that aren't my own, but his. Moments at the hospital where I feel as if he's asking for my help. I may just be imagining them. Manifesting my wishful thinking into my reality."

MARIANA TOOK A GLANCE AT HER. "Maybe he's asking you to let him go."

Olivia's expression changed to disgust.

"Why would you say that?" she asked.

"He's dying Olivia. Borden's speaking to you, asking you for help. To let him move on. He lives inside of you now. You have to understand that."

Olivia couldn't believe the words coming out of Mariana's mouth.

"I need to be at the hospital! How can you say those things to me? I have to go. I'm late. Lock up after you leave!" Olivia shouted, grabbing her things.

"I'm sorry, but I love Borden too, and he's just suffering." She said. "And sure, I'm just going to use the restroom and I'll head out." She replied.

"I'll talk to you about this later," Olivia said with disappointment, closing the door in anger.

Mariana watched her drive away through the shades.

OLIVIA FELT guilty for how their conversation ended as she drove down the road, so she reached for her phone to apologize. However, it rang for a while without an answer.

Come on.

She dialed again.

The phone continued to ring.

"Hello?" Mariana answered.

"Mom, hello?"

"Yeah, hi honey."

"Mom, why do you sound asleep?"

"Because I was. It's early."

Olivia slammed her brakes.

"MOM! Where are you? What do you mean? Stop joking around." She demanded.

"Is everything okay? I'm at home. In fact, I was worried about you. You didn't come home last night. I figured you stayed at the hospital." She replied.

"No, I stayed at my house. We just talked?"

"Olivia, I'm at home. I prayed all night for you and Angi."

Olivia's face flushed.

"I have to go," Olivia said.

"Wait, is everything okay?"

"Yeah, everything's fine."

"Okay honey, love you."

"Love you too."

OLIVIA HUNG up and sat in silence. She adjusted her rearview mirror to metaphorically look back at her house, and at whatever was that person that came to visit.

Was her car in the driveway? Damn! I don't know. I left so fast I didn't notice. Maybe she's messing with me? If she's not? What was that?

Her skin was crawling. Her mouth was dry.

She said she was praying for me and Angi.

"Angi!" she exclaimed.

She called him Angi.

At the house, the only name she kept using was Borden. That wasn't my mom.

The radio, my mom? Was that even my mom? She spoke so cruelly at the end about Borden. She would never want me to give up on Borden. She was praying for us! For him! That's not someone that would want me to let him go.

I'm being misled. Tricked. Whoever that was, they're not going to succeed. I spoke to a ghost. That's insane. An actual ghost. In my mother's image! What the hell is that? An eidolon?

SHE IGNITED the engine and burned rubber as she skidded onto the road again, trailblazing towards the hospital.

AT THE HOUSE, Mariana, who had spoken with Olivia that morning, calmly approached the radio. Without having to plug it back in, she stared at it, and the song began to play.

"That's a good song," she said, moments before dissipating into thin air.

12

RUDE AWAKENING

Olivia, if you can hear me. Please, don't let me go.

Over at the house, Borden had transformed the place into a complete construction site, with hammers striking walls, tables, and anything else he set his eyes on. Olivia arrived amidst the chaos.

"Just what the hell are you doing?" Olivia questioned.

Borden couldn't hear her. He was wearing earmuffs, breaking apart a piece of furniture.

"Borden!" she shouted. "Borden!"

Finally, she moved around his destruction and into his line of sight. She gestured for him to remove his ear muffs.

"What are you doing?" she screamed.

"I know this looks bad, but hear me out," Borden replied.

Olivia's mood had already boiled. She didn't like this one bit.

"Have you gone mad?" she exclaimed.

"No, that's the funny part. Look, just look. Come here for a second."

He guides her over to a pile of debris.

"You see this? Just wait. Trust me."

"Borden, there are holes in the wall!"

"I know, I know, just look. Look at this."

He points to the junk on the floor. "Any second now," he said.

Olivia, annoyed, humored Borden. She gazed at a piece of furniture that was slowly but surely rebuilding itself.

"I don't understand," she said.

"Isn't that wild? The whole thing is just being destroyed in reverse. Olivia, that's not all. Everything in here is the same. It's like magic!" he cried out maniacally.

"Borden, what's going on?"

"That's what I would like to know. Here, come to the kitchen."

They rushed over as Borden held her hand. Borden pulled a ceramic bowl from the cupboard and held it over the floor.

"Watch this."

"Borden no!"

Crash!

The bowl shattered into pieces. Olivia was livid.

"Borden! Why would you do that?"

"Wait, check this out," Borden stated, gleaming from cheek to cheek.

He opened the cupboard and pulled out the same ceramic bowl.

"Ta-da! It's magic!"

"This shouldn't be possible," Olivia remarked.

"No, it shouldn't. Finally, we agree on something," Borden replied.

"Okay, so now what?"

"Now what? Olivia, everything we break just appears anew or rebuilds itself. Remember what we talked about on the porch? Feeling like we were in a movie. Well now, it feels like that, but with special powers."

Olivia seemed uncomfortable once more.

"Borden, I thought we were going to focus on our trip."

"Screw the trip! Don't you think this is worth talking about? Why don't you call your mom? I bet she would get a kick out of it. Look, look! That hole in the wall. Back to normal! Isn't that something?" Borden ran around like a madman.

"I don't want to call her about this?"

"Why not?"

"Because I–"

"–can't?" Borden ominously interjected.

Olivia stood quietly.

"You can't call her. Want to know why? Because I tried already. There's no line. We don't exist here. This place doesn't exist here, Olivia!"

"Borden, you're talking crazy again. I think maybe you should–"

"–Should what? Go for a walk? Clear my head? Let's do that. Actually, that's a fantastic idea, Olivia." he shouted.

Olivia began to appear afraid of Borden.

"You're scaring me, Borden. Why are you doing this?" she cried out.

"Let's go for a walk. Oh, wait, we can't. I tried that too. I ran into an invisible wall. Felt like a mime on a street corner in Rome. Can you explain that?" Borden demanded. "Then, I dug a hole. I thought to myself, maybe I can dig underneath whatever the hell was blocking my path. That's right, you guessed it. Hit the imaginary wall again. I can't seem to leave this place, even if I wanted to. So tell me, Olivia, if that's your real name. What should I do?"

OLIVIA DIDN'T KNOW what to say. She appeared emotionally hurt by Borden's actions.

"Stop pretending already!"

"Pretending what?" she replied, tears in her eyes.

"The watch, Olivia!" he screamed. "The watch is not broken. It's missing the engraving. The only cereal in the house is the one we hate. You sat in the wrong chair. You didn't notice that I was in the wrong chair as well. You never call out of work." Borden screamed, his voice beginning to break.

Borden's heart rate began to increase. He's becoming too stimulated. Too emotional.

"You called me Borden. Not Angier."

"What are you talking about?" Olivia innocently replied.

"Please. Stop. I've seen too much shit by now. You being another one of those dreams or hallucinations wouldn't surprise me. Whatever you are, nice try. But you're not my Olivia. You will never be her."

Borden wore his vulnerability like armor, coated with temporary courage. He didn't want to go this far, but he had no alternative choice. He had to put all of his cards on the table.

Olivia cried. That's all that she did. She slid down the

wall she was leaning on until she sat on the floor. Her head was buried in her knees. She cried.

Borden held his ground. He remained visibly stern in his accusations. It was difficult to witness her like this for him. He fought every fiber of his being to apologize and comfort her.

His headache began to get stronger.

No, not now. Please. Not now.

Olivia continued to cry as Borden tended to his pain.

Her cry slowed down.

Crocodile tears?

Olivia's head still buried between her knees, she began to chuckle.

She's laughing. Why? Oh shit. What did I get myself into?

Her head lifted slowly, her eyes still hidden from his. The laughing intensified. Borden's heart rate began to elevate once more. The headache blindsided him in agony. Olivia laughed hysterically now, as Borden cowered on the floor. He tried to fight the pain and look over at Olivia, but he was afraid of what he saw.

"You stubborn fool," Olivia remarked, but with a deeper voice.

Borden in pain, conflicted about where he can divert his attention, tried to listen and stay alert.

"It was so simple. For some reason, you can't seem to detach yourself from this pointless world. She seems to be the only reason we can't leave yet. How long can she keep that up, though? Days? Months? Years? In the meantime, you'll be here, living the same day over and over. How delusional must you be in thinking you can get out of this? You only delay the inevitable. You prolong your misery. Sooner or later, she's going to give up on you. She'll cut the ties that keep you here. Then I'll show up and collect your sad remains. We're already late enough as it is. No matter. I'll be here to pick up your pieces. Willingly or not, you're coming with me," Olivia screamed, laughing at her last words.

Borden heard every word. His pain, however, and his jadedness to irrational scenarios distracted him from the message. He was blacking out toward the last half of it. His eyes were closing; he saw Olivia, blink after blink, until she was no longer in the room with him. He conceded to the pain. Darkness once more has taken him.

"Hello?"

Silence. Darkness.

"Hello, is anyone there?" Borden asked.

It was as if he were sealed inside a box - a casket; he imagined - unable to see anything. He had grown accustomed to waking up in different places every time his headaches struck and blacked him out. Now, he waited for a new person or thing to heed his vague warnings.

"Hello? Anyone here? It's Borden," he shouted.

As if that would change anything.

"Borden?"

"Yes! Hello, who's there?"

A soft voice broke the silence again.

"Daisy."

Borden took a moment to reply.

Daisy? Who's Daisy? Why does that name sound so familiar? For once, someone is actually answering me. Who is Daisy?

"Hello, are you there Borden?" Daisy asked.

"Sorry, yes, I'm here. Remind me,"

"Ah, you can't see me, right?" she said with joy in her voice.

"No, I can't. I'm sorry. I can't recall the name."

"I was worried for a second there," she said.

"Why, why were you worried?" He asked.

"For Olivia, sweetie."

Borden's stomach dropped. Hearing his wife's name.

"You know Olivia?"

"Well, of course, she was my doctor."

Borden's memory of her returned.

"Daisy!" he exclaimed. "Daisy! You're Olivia's patient. You loved that, that pudding! Right?"

"Yes, that's right," she replied.

"What are you doing here?"

"It's time to go," she replied. "The boatman is waiting for me."

"The boatman?" Borden replied.

"Yes, he's here to take me."

"No, you can't go! Don't go with him," he pleaded.

"It's my time, sweetie. It's okay. You can't see me, right? That's because you're not ready. That's why I was worried about Olivia. I thought she lost you."

"Where are we, Daisy? I can't see anything. I can hear you though," he said.

"The docks. My spirit guide brought me here, for the boatman to carry me out."

"Spirit guide?" Borden asked.

"Yes. My spirit guide looked like my husband. Oh, how I miss him. He came to me in my dreams while I lay in the hospital. He'd visit my room sometimes. He helped me transition here to the docks. Of course, I learned it wasn't my husband. The guide said it would make things easier to understand," Daisy said with comfort in her voice.

"I don't have a spirit guide–"

Borden bit his tongue, recalling the Olivia he's been dealing with.

"–wait, I think I do have one."

"But you're not fully crossed yet, Borden. I don't think you should be here. I don't know how you are," Daisy remarked.

"I don't know either, but my, I think, my spirit guide, took the appearance of Olivia. I've been experiencing so many kinds of hideous and sinister things."

"That doesn't sound like a spirit guide."

"Did your spirit guide ever get violent towards you?" Borden asked.

"Violent? No. They explained why they were there. Told me what was going to happen. I felt peace, actually." Daisy said.

Borden took a moment to think about the Olivia that he's been living with. The visions he's been having felt more like spirit guides than she did. Though for the first time, Borden felt like he has a plan of action. A sense of direction.

"It seems as though time is of the essence. Whatever connection you seem to have with Olivia, you must make it stronger. Otherwise, your body will just become weaker in this place, and you'll be here at the docks."

"How can I reach out to her?" Borden asked.

"I remember seeing Bill in reflections, mostly. Probably why I liked the vanilla pudding so much. It was tasty, but in the end, I would lick the spoon clean and he would be there. Calling me. Letting me know that my time was coming to an end. I think he sent the spirit guide in his image. He was always so thoughtful. Now, I'll get to see him soon."

"Reflections. A mirror?"

"That could work. From what it seems, you got one foot in the door. Please, for Olivia's sake—that poor girl—keep that foot out."

Daisy took a breath, the sound of a woman content with what life had given her and ready to face what lay ahead. The final frontier.

"I have to go now. The boatman is waiting. Wish I could give you one last hug. You were always so nice. See you soon, but not too soon, Borden."

"Goodbye Daisy. Thank you."

BORDEN RETURNED TO SILENCE.

He couldn't see anything, but his mind was racing with thoughts and ideas. He began to scheme, trying to come up with a way to communicate with Olivia from wherever he was. He was certain that he wasn't in the afterlife, nor was he amongst the living, as Daisy had confirmed.

I'm in the middle. I'm in the waiting room of a hospital. I'm neither alive nor dead. The boatman is the doctor and I'm the patient. How do I cancel my appointment?

Olivia, if you can hear me. Please, don't let me go.

13

THE PLEDGE

Don't get so snappy with me, mortal.

The hospital was in mourning. Olivia stood at the reception desk on arrival. Three candles were on display, with a laminated piece of paper leaning on a vase holding the most beautiful assortment of flowers. Olivia was still shaken, but this message flipped her world upside down.

Olivia felt lost and alone, not knowing where to turn or what to do next. She clutched the flowers tightly in her hand as if they were a lifeline, keeping her tethered to reality.

Dear friends and family,
We ask that you join us in mourning the

loss of Daisy Raquel Willonette. This area will be quiet for the remainder of the day in honor of Daisy. Please try to be mindful. Thank you.

OLIVIA'S TEARS trailed the contours of her face and fell onto the counter.

When? When did this happen? Last night? When did she leave us?

Olivia guided her attention to the flowers. She smiled, thinking about her.

"Daisies. How fitting."

Sarah, the receptionist, slid her chair over towards Olivia and gave her a woeful smile. Olivia returned the gesture. They began to whisper.

"When?" she asked.

Sarah replied, "In the middle of the night."

"Was there anything we could've done?"

"No," Sarah said, "she had a nocturnal death."

"I see. That's rare." Olivia replied.

"Well," Sarah recalled, "she was rare, herself."

"That she was. She definitely was. I hope she's in a better place now."

"I'm sure she is," Sarah said.

"I'm sorry I was late. I couldn't sleep last night." Olivia confessed.

"Don't worry about it. It hasn't been a hectic morning, so you're okay. Borden hasn't had any new issues." Sarah said, leaning closer to Olivia.

Hearing about Borden's condition put Olivia at ease.

"That's good news. I'm gonna go get ready and hit the floors."

"See you then," Sarah replied.

WALKING into the locker room felt unsettling as she recalled the encounter she had with that unidentifiable man. The fluorescent lights flickered overhead, casting an eerie glow on the lockers. She could feel the cool metal of her locker handle as she turned it, the sound of the latch clicking open and echoing in the empty room. Her skin prickled with goosebumps as she recalled the man's words, praising the paper boat and mentioning the paper crane.

Did he come for Daisy? He would knock at her window, or so she said. Is the boatman coming for Borden now? Is it his turn?

Olivia grabbed the paper boat from her locker. She fiddled with it.

This appeared on Daisy's bedside table. She didn't know where it came from. It couldn't have just appeared. Someone placed it there. Something placed it there.

If this boat was placed there, it means that this person or thing can interact with this world. What kind of message is it trying to send? Is this the boatman's calling card? Some weird supernatural killer?

If the boatman exists wherever Borden is, then is it possible to communicate with Borden? It sounds absurd, but the evidence is in this tiny paper boat. It was strategically placed. It appeared out of thin air. Like a magic trick.

"I SEE you still have the little boat."

Olivia's body went cold, turning her attention to that despicable-looking old man.

"You!" she screamed.

"You remember me?" the old man replied.

"Who are you? You don't work here," she called.

"No. You're right. I don't," he said, "I look pretty good in this outfit though, don't you think?"

Olivia placed the boat in her locker and shut it. The old man laughed at the sight of it.

"Are you the boatman?" Olivia asked, gulping to maintain her courage.

"Me?" the old man asked, bringing his arms to his chest. "No, I'm not the boatman. That's a funny name, 'the boatman,' sounds spooky. No, I'm definitely not the boatman."

"Were you at my house this morning?" Olivia asked, shivering at the thought.

"No? Now how would that even be possible?" he asked, moving closer to Olivia. "I'm a janitor lady. I just take out the trash," he said, grinning with glee.

"Bullshit."

"What gave it away?" he asked.

"Borden. Mariana doesn't call him Borden," she replied.

"Very perceptive. I underestimated your cleverness. Either that or I dropped the ball on that one. I technically am a janitor, though. I just pick up different kinds of trash," he said, laughing at his own joke.

"You're an eidolon," she said, taking subtle steps backward.

"You can call it that. Kind of. I suppose. No, you see, I work for the so-called 'boatman,' and you're making my job a little harder than I'd like it to be," he said.

"Your job?"

"Yes, my job. Borden is my job." He said in an annoyed tone. "Not too long ago, it was that old lady."

"Daisy!" she exclaimed.

"Woah, Daisy, my apologies. It's nothing personal, it's strictly business. Borden's as good as dead. For some reason, his soul is latched onto this realm and I can't understand why." he said, "Meeting you however, I forget how long ago–time works differently here than at the docks–the point is, Borden is somehow still tethered and I'd like to facilitate the issue by cutting him loose. If his time in-between runs out, and he's still attached, he's not gonna have a good time. I'm doing you guys a favor."

"Borden's not going anywhere. I don't care what you're here for, clearly, you can't just take him, otherwise, you wouldn't be here." Olivia said.

A SUDDEN SHIFT of power between the two. Olivia found a chink in the armor. She realized that whatever this was; it wasn't strong enough to do what it wanted. Her fear turned to anger. Turned to strength.

"Instead, you rely on parlor tricks. Foolish attempts to encourage me to let him go. It was you, wasn't it?" Olivia said.

The old man sported an annoyed expression, agitated at her cleverness. He refused to acknowledge her conclusions.

"Not so talkative anymore huh," Olivia said.

The lights flickered, and the man is no longer in front of her.

"More tricks. Okay." Olivia said with confidence.

"Don't get so snappy with me, mortal," he said, appearing behind her. "You'll start giving me new ideas. It's only a matter of time. He's weak, and he grows weaker. Soon he'll accept his fate, and your hold on him won't be strong enough to keep him here. You're wasting your time. He's mine," he said, his breath lingering in her ear.

The lights flickered again and the cackling of the old man echoed in the locker room.

He was gone.

OLIVIA, alone once more, opened her locker. She's afraid but also curious. She grabbed the paper boat.

He didn't leave that boat. He's not the boatman. Who left the boat? Who would?–

The most obvious clue she overlooked was one she hadn't thought of before.

"The paper crane! Magic! It had to be!" she yelled.

She began to unfold the boat.

Her mouth plummeted to the ground before her body did.

"It can't be."

Her hand covered her mouth out of disbelief.

It was a letter. A message.

"It was you all along. How did I miss this? Oh, Borden. Only you could manage something this insane. You truly are magic." She cried.

She gripped the paper firmly, brought it to her pursed lips, and clutched it into her chest.

I can't believe it. I can't believe it.

She read:

Olivia, I hope this reaches you. First and foremost...

TEARS FELL onto the paper as she finished. She folded it into a tiny square and places it in her pocket. Her sobs were heard throughout the locker room.

I'LL GET YOU BACK. I promise.

14

THE MESSENGER

Every decision I've made. Every encounter. How do I know what wasn't or was planned to occur?

Borden paced back and forth in his living room, his mind consumed by a newfound sense of clarity. Finally, he could focus on a plan. His goal was to establish communication so he could find out where he was and why he was there.

"Daisy talked about reflections. She would see her husband in spoons, in windows. In mirrors!" He shouted.

He suddenly remembered the mirror in his office, the one he had used to travel into that strange dimension where the sea was red as blood. That same mirror had also caused strange distortions in his hallway before that.

It had clearly served as a gateway for Borden.

"I was right about that mirror! We never owned that. Somehow it was placed here, for me to use! To find my way out of here!"

"There is no way out of here!" Olivia shouted, standing in the corner of the room.

BORDEN SHIFTED his gaze over to her, as she walked her way over to the couch and took a seat.

"When will you realize that there's no getting out of here?" She asked.

"I'll figure it out." Borden replied with determination, focused on his planning that he wrote down in his journal.

"It's a waste of time, really. Time that you're soon not going to have."

"Why are you even here? Your cover's blown. No point in pretending to be Olivia." Borden said.

"But it's kind of fun! I like being her–sounding like her– I think you should just stop this nonsense and just come with me." She said.

"Go with you?"

Olivia nodded.

"Go with you where, exactly? The docks?"

Olivia became interested in the conversation.

"The docks? You know about the docks?" She asked with surprise.

"Yeah, I know all about the docks."

Olivia began to cry.

"You know about that? It was supposed to be a surprise, Borden!" she said, mocking him with fake tears.

Borden is annoyed at her antics. Olivia noticed that Borden wasn't biting at her taunts. She moved in closer to him as he wrote.

"She's giving up on you, you know that right?" She said.

Borden didn't reply.

"Tsk.tsk.tsk. I was just with her, and she agreed with me that maybe she should just give up." She said callously.

"What do you mean you were with her?" He asked.

"Ah! There he is. I struck a nerve," she replied, moving away as Borden became defensive.

Borden waited for his answer.

"Let's just say she had a little chat with your mother-in-law. You see, Mariana feels differently about you, and she might've encouraged her to let you go," she said with a taunting smile.

"You took her image? She wouldn't fall for that. Not Olivia."

"Time will tell I suppose."

"Yeah, it will."

"Just a reminder, time doesn't work the way you think it does, Borden. As far as you know, she might've made up her mind weeks ago. Maybe even years." She said.

"Leave me alone." Borden demanded.

"Would you feel more comfortable if I looked like you?" She asked, shifting into an exact copy of Borden.

Borden's eyes widened as he came face to face with another version of himself. Out of frustration, he threw his journal at him, shouting, "I said, leave me alone!"

EIDOLON DISAPPEARED, leaving Borden panting and gasping for air. He was becoming too overwhelmed, feeling his headache starting to take hold. He focused on calming himself down before it became too much to handle.

I need to stay calm. I can't have another headache right now. I need to focus.

He picked up his tossed journal, dusting it off and placing it on the coffee table. In an attempt to relax, he turned to his radio and flicked it on.

"Jimi." he said.

He referred to Jimi Hendrix. The song "All Along The Watchtower" was playing on the radio.

It played for a while before it suddenly cut off. Borden's head lifted from the couch. He was pleasantly enjoying it with his eyes closed.

What the hell?

He flicked it back on.

Before he could sit back down, the music was turned off again.

Okay what's going on.

He pressed the power button with an angered intensity, making it seem as if it were the radio's fault.

He didn't make it to the couch this time. Immediately, the radio's power cord ripped itself out of the outlet.

No time for relaxation I guess. Fuck this place. I need to get out.

Borden's had enough. He's jaded to the point where this just strikes him as an inconvenience.

Stepping into his office, he had one goal in mind. The mirror. He had to figure out how it worked the last time. It somehow managed to transport him out to the middle of the sea.

I was just staring at it. What was I thinking about?

He faced the mirror. So far it was just his reflection. A normal mirror.

Come on. There has to be something.

He made a few weak attempts at surprising the mirror by either closing his eyes and opening them, or jumping into the frame.

No luck.

A picture of Olivia caught his eye. He thought about her and how he wished he was with her. How he used to visit her at the hospital to drop off a snack or for the sake of just seeing her.

The mirror began to ripple! The lights began to shine!

Borden noticed.

"It's happening. The ripples. The mirror is swirling!" he exclaimed.

The lights in his office began to fizzle in and out as if the mirror was drawing their energy. The mirror's aura became stronger. Borden, staring at the center of the whirlpool in the mirror, took a moment to gather his courage.

"Here goes nothing," he said, diving straight into the mirror.

Flashes of light surrounded him as he fell through what seemed like a portal, like a skydiver, except the world around him was composed of a plethora of images. As he fell, he saw brief images of his life, like memories being replayed. His body was absorbed by one of those images.

Borden felt like he was being pulled in different directions, disoriented and dizzy. The feeling was as if he had just been spun around in circles. But slowly, his senses returned, and he realized that he had made it through the mirror. He looked around in awe, trying to make sense of the scene before him.

I did it.

I'm in the hospital. I did it.

The first thing that caught his attention was the sound of beeping machines. They were coming from all directions, and their rhythm seemed to synchronize with his heartbeat. He could also smell the faint scent of antiseptic in the air, and it reminded him of the times he had been in the hospital before.

I actually did it!

I'm sitting in a waiting room?

That's when Borden looked down at his hands.

"These aren't my hands. These aren't my legs?"

Panic began to set in. He had managed to travel to the hospital, but not as himself. He was operating someone else's body, like a vessel.

"No, no, what now? How is this possible?" Borden wondered aloud.

As a young man walked past with a paper in his hand, Borden's eyes followed him to his seat. Astonished, Borden couldn't look away. The young man took a seat next to him and began fidgeting with his piece of paper.

Finally tearing his gaze away, Borden looked around, confused by his surroundings.

"This can't be possible. What have I done? That's...that's me?"

The young man looked over at Borden and gave an uncomfortable smile. Borden tried to calm down and be as normal as he could given the circumstance. He couldn't fathom the idea that he was sitting next to his past self.

Borden attempted to break the ice, and asked the young man what he was doing.

"A crane." he replied without moving his gaze away from the paper.

Incredible. That's exactly what I said?

Borden's face was filled with confusion. The young man mistook Borden's expression to be related to his folding of the paper.

"Trust the process," the young man said.

I said that. I told that man to trust the process. This man. Why am I this man?

Borden, shell-shocked at how this was even possible, tried his hardest to pretend that he was in fact that man. He remembered word for word the piece of advice that the man had given him.

Did I suggest to myself to give Olivia the crane? After all these years, what I thought was a strange interaction that led to one of the greatest things that ever happened to me, was fabricated? It was planned all along? It wasn't fate. It was me. I suggested young Borden should deliver that crane to Olivia. I set myself on this course.

The conversation went exactly as it did in the past.

"What do they call you, sir? The love guru?"

Borden on the verge of tears, realizing how everything all at once was connected, tried to respond to the boy.

"Something about you makes me feel at ease, sir. You have very nice energy." the young man said.

"Thank you." he replied, struggling to recall his name. "You can call me Bob. How about you?"

"Borden. The name's Borden." the young Borden replied.

I've traveled, back in time, to direct myself towards Olivia. Has the future already therefore happened? If it was me from the beginning, it was the future me talking to me that day?Everything is planned. Is this destiny?

. . .

BORDEN'S HEART rate was elevating. This moment became too much for him. His headache started slowly, but increased rapidly.

"What's wrong, Bob? You okay?" the young Borden asked.

"Yeah, I'm fine–" he replied. "Say, when you give that to that special girl of yours, you should add a little note to it. They love that. Makes them feel even more magical. Better yet, you should write a secret message inside it, so that if one day she was curious to unfold it, she would be surprised again. A gift within a gift."

"That's a genius idea actually! It shouldn't take too long to make another one anyway, I'll do that. What do you think I should add?" the young Borden asked.

The headache was coming in and Borden was having difficulty ignoring it.

This might be a long shot, but I need Olivia to try anything and everything.

"Write whatever you'd like, maybe she'll read it in a week, or maybe in one hundred years, so keep that in mind." Borden replied, rubbing his temples.

"Are you sure you're okay?"

"Yes, how about this: if there's something special you want to wish for, Add this crane to a pile of 999 or more."

"Is that real?"

"Well, probably not. In Japanese legend, the crane or Senbazuru, 1,000 cranes, there's a belief that if a person made 1,000 paper cranes they would be granted a wish."

I could sure use a wish right now though.

"Who has time to make 1,000 cranes?" the young man asked, laughing at the thought.

"It does seem a bit excessive. The crane alone though, is well spirited. It's a token of good fortune."

"Okay, I suppose," he said, unfolding the paper as he spoke.

"And sign it of course. With your full name."

"I'm not a big fan of my full name. It's the reason I use my last name. Borden." he replied.

"Ah! More the reason to do it. No where else, would your name be signed in full on a personal letter."

"Angier Borden? Like that?" he asked, moving the paper in Borden's direction.

"Like that. See. Now make the crane again!" Borden said, fighting the urge to massage his head.

"Sir are you sure you're okay? I mean, we're at the hospital. I can grab someone for you."

"No it's okay"—

THE PAIN WAS TOO MUCH, he let out a horrifying scream and his vision blurred to black. The young Borden's shouts became inaudible to Borden, as if he was suddenly a million yards away from the young man.

The immense pressure and weight of falling through time and space returned. The sensation of falling overtook him and the strobing lights and memories were back. Moments after, he was spat out and laid on the ground of his office, wet and gasping for air.

"I'M BACK. I'm back here." he said.

Squirming on the floor, he was relieved to be back at the house. Still, it wasn't his house though. He sat up, coughing and catching his breath.

The mirror worked. It just didn't work the way I was hoping it would.

"Every decision I've made. Every encounter. How do I know what wasn't or was planned to occur?"

Borden's realization that the idea of everything being pre-programmed, coded to exist in a specific way, was daunting. Regardless if he were behind his past life's decisions, or therefore a future experience being manipulated before it had even happened, he was glad that it led to Olivia. It was a lot for him to take in.

What else was I a part of? I need to figure out how this thing works. How did I end up in someone else's body, specifically in that year? Maybe it was meant to happen. If I didn't travel there, maybe I never would've met Olivia. Everything, all of this, had to happen. It's part of the plan. I need to find my way out.

BORDEN ROSE to his feet and fixed his gaze on the mirror, which had returned to its normal state. He knew that this mirror was capable of traversing different realms, and even time itself. Taking a deep breath, he closed his eyes and visualized Olivia.

As Borden focused on his destination and the body he wished to inhabit, the air in the room started to feel charged, and a gust of wind picked up. It seemed to radiate from the mirror and grew stronger with each passing second. The wind grew to a howling gale, causing papers to fly off his desk and knocking over small objects.

As the wind intensified, the mirror began to ripple and shimmer, as if it were alive. The lights flickered and dimmed, before shining brighter than before. The magnetic pull was palpable, and Borden felt as if he were being pulled toward the mirror. It was as if the mirror had a life of its own, and it was using all of its power to set Borden's course of destination.

. . .

In that chaotic moment, a gleam in Borden's eye reflected back to the mirror. A smirk on his face.

Now, let's try this again.

15

THE TROJAN HORSE

"It's time Borden, time for the docks!"

It felt strange not having Daisy around anymore. Olivia sat on the now-empty bed in Patient Room B, reminiscing about the moments she shared with Daisy. The pudding was a given, but what she thought about the most were the conversations they had.

Daisy would share stories about Mariana and how similar Olivia was to her mother. The stories about her husband Bill were hilarious; she always portrayed him as some type of troublemaker, which reminded Olivia of Borden. Of course, Bill had long passed, and Daisy didn't have any family left. However, Olivia treated her like family, and she hoped that the feeling was mutual. She loved Daisy, and she was sure that Daisy loved her too.

She felt terrible for not being there when it happened, but she had a feeling that Daisy was in a better place now.

ACCORDING to the letter from Borden that Olivia had discovered hidden under the guise of a paper boat, Daisy was indeed in a better place - the docks. To Olivia, it sounded like a nasty place, considering that "the boatman" was involved. Olivia had her fair share of interactions with him that made her feel that way. However, she accepted that it made sense and that it didn't seem personal to the people who traveled beyond. But part of her couldn't fully accept that it wasn't personal to her.

It was surreal for Olivia to acknowledge that the after-life was a real place, and that Borden was somehow close to it. She looked over the note once more.

Olivia, I hope this reaches you,

First and foremost I want to tell you that I love you. I always will. No matter what.

What I'm about to tell you is going to be very hard to believe, but I hope you can trust me when I say that it will all make sense in the end...

There was a knock at the open door.

"What is that sweetie," Mariana said, entering the room.

Olivia folded the piece of paper and stashed it in her pocket.

"Mom, you're here." Olivia said.

"I came as fast as I could after you called."

"Yeah, sorry about that. I didn't mean to wake you."

Mariana gave her a look of understanding. She took a seat besides her on the bed.

"You said, we spoke. When?" Mariana asked.

"I don't know mom, things are just really weird. I don't even know where to start." Olivia replied.

"Well, how's Angi doing?"

Olivia smiled upon hearing that name. Then she remembered how credible Eidolon's image of Mariana had been and felt knots in her stomach thinking about it. She found it strange that Mariana hadn't asked about Daisy yet, considering they had a history as well. This paranoia led to her next line of questioning.

"HEY MOM."

"What is it honey?" Mariana asked.

"I'm sorry about Daisy, I'm sure you read the note at the desk. We lost her."

"I did, I did read that. I'm sorry too." Mariana said, bowing her head in sorrow.

Olivia analyzed her closely, and continued.

"I wish I had a chance to get her a last cup of pudding."

"Oh, yeah. The pudding, she loved that stuff."

"She couldn't have enough of that Choco—"

Mariana's head snapped upon hearing that and interrupted Olivia. 'Chocolate? Sweetie, no. Remember, it was vanilla. Have you been getting her chocolate this whole time? Oh, poor Ms. Daisy. How could you? I told you to always get the vanilla pudding!' Mariana exclaimed.

Olivia was relieved to hear that.

Yeah, that's my mom. Good.

. . .

"I'M JUST KIDDING, it was always the vanilla pudding." Olivia replied.

"Good. I'll pray for her when I go home. She knew about the pudding by the way." Mariana said, a smirk on her face.

"What do you mean?"

"Please, don't act so innocent. We knew what you were up to."

Olivia nudged her mom's shoulder, asking for her to elaborate what she meant. "Come on, tell me."

"THE PUDDING. You would occasionally run into her room and steal her pudding cup."

"I did not!" Olivia scoffed.

"She would see you, but would pretend to be asleep because she thought it was so cute." Mariana added.

"Did she really? Oh, now I feel awful!" Olivia confessed.

"No, don't. It made her day. And that made mine. Seeing little Olivia run around and interact with my patients. I was always worried that you'd resent me for having you here, wasting away your childhood." Mariana said, sadness in her voice.

"Don't be crazy mom, I loved those years of my life. You and this building helped nurture me to be who I am today. It's where I met Borden too." Olivia said with a smile.

Mariana teared up upon hearing her daughter say such nice things. The last thing a parent wants to hear is of their shortcomings as a mother or father, and the fear of being hated for it. Olivia's affirmation that it was the opposite made for a tender moment between the two of them.

. . .

MARIANA CAME UP WITH AN IDEA.

"Why don't we share a vanilla pudding in her honor? I'm sure Ms. Daisy will look down on us and smile knowing the tradition of the infamous vanilla pudding would live inside of us now." Mariana suggested.

Olivia nodded in agreement, though her thoughts wandered to where Daisy actually was: the docks. She was currently waiting for the boatman, and while the thought was scary, the way Borden had mentioned it in the letter made it seem okay. It was a transition - that was all - to a better place. A better place for those who were ready to move on.

Olivia feigned a smile and said, "let's do it!"

The two of them walked together towards the cafeteria.

BACK AT THE house in the realm of the transitioning souls, Borden faced his mirror. Charged and with a destination ready to go, his body disappeared leaving behind the usual puddle.

At that precise moment, Eidolon had arrived to further antagonize Borden. It still took on the image of his wife.

"Hello? Borden? Where are you? What are you up to?" He asked.

There was no response. He approached the office and noticed the dripping on the wall beneath the mirror.

"Interesting." He said. "Just what do you think you're doing?"

The mirror swirled with a faint image of the hospital in the center of the rippling rings.

"The hospital huh? I see you learned how to traverse

the realms. I'm quite impressed." Eidolon said, taking a runner's stance in front of the mirror.

"Unfortunately for you, this is child's play for me!"

Eidolon lunged straight into the mirror.

BORDEN TRAVELED through the currents of time with determination. The lights didn't faze him this time. The memories and images that flashed alongside him didn't distract him from his goal. He was focused. Laser focused.

HE ARRIVED.

He was in a room.

There was a delay in his vision before he could fully see. Similar to the last time he traveled through the mirror.

I made it. I'm at the hospital. This room? It feels familiar.

A little dizzy from the fall, he stumbled to his feet. The machinery beeped and the linoleum floors were cold. The smell of a sterile environment attacked his senses. He saw a bed and someone was in it.

Is that?

The cotton hair and wrinkled skin gave it away.

"Daisy?" he said to himself.

She was asleep in her bed. He clearly missed the mark once more. He made it to the hospital but if Daisy was still there, it meant that she hadn't passed yet.

Damn it, not again. I'm not at the right time. That doesn't mean that Olivia isn't here though. I need to find her and speak to her.

. . .

As Borden got closer to her bed, she began to shift her weight around. Her eyes, were barely visible, but they opened. They looked at Borden. He didn't know how to react.

"Borden? Borden? Is that you? How is this possible?" she asked.

"What do you mean?"

"You're in the other room? You're okay now? Olivia must be thrilled," she said, struggling to finish her sentences.

She felt like she was dreaming. Hallucinating even. Once she came closer to consciousness, the situation became alarming.

"Borden! Borden!" she shouted. "Borden!"

The machines began to beep recklessly and the stomping of a few doctors running into the room startled Borden.

He felt the strangest sensation when one managed to run through his body.

"They can't see me? Why?" he asked himself.

I don't have a body here? Daisy said I was in the other room?

"Borden! Borden!" Daisy shouted, over and over again.

Borden fed his curiosity and left the room, eager to find the Olivia from this timeline.

Walking across the hallway something drew his attention over his left shoulder. He turned his head slowly and saw into the room through the viewing window. It was his body.

It's me? Why am I there?

He tilted his head up to the title on the door. It read: **Patient Room D**

I'm a patient? Why am I a patient? Am I dying? Is that why I'm in this mess?

The graveyard, the sea, the corpses, the fake Olivia—none of that had prepared him to stand before his own lifeless body. An influx of emotions generated within him. He was Olivia's patient. This whole time. He's been her patient. He reached out his hand to touch the Borden that lay on the bed, but it was rejected like trying to combine the wrong ends of a magnet.

This entire time? The voices I heard in the dreams, the blackouts, the computer, they must have belonged to the people in this room that spoke around me. Or to me. Olivia must've been behind those messages! 'Don't go Borden, not yet.' How did I miss this? How did I not think about this. I'm trapped in my subconscious. Their words were able to reach me! The faceless nurse, warning me about the fake Olivia, my own subconscious was trying to defend me!

OUTSIDE IN THE HALLWAY, Olivia was brought to Patient Room B where Daisy was located. The doctors that rushed to Daisy's aid heard her cries for Borden, so they brought Olivia in as soon as possible. Borden didn't notice her as he was too distracted by his own body.

SHORTLY AFTER, a strange magnetism pulled Borden's attention toward Daisy's room.

An emergency in there? Everyone's running inside! What's going on?

He turned back to his body and gave it one last look. "I'll be right back."

As he exited the room, he noticed a barrage of doctors and nurses were running to Daisy's room.

This must be when she died?

He followed behind one of the doctors into the room and stopped dead in his tracks when he saw who they were rushing over to.

It was Olivia.

She was on the floor, crying and screaming.

Borden was shocked to see her that way. One particular person wasn't stooping down. His gaze made contact with that person. It was Eidolon.

"Hi Borden. Fancy seeing you here." He said, morphing into the spitting image of his wife.

The doctors continued to scream and shout, "Olivia! Olivia!"

Borden watched in horror, he felt helpless.

"Stop it! Whatever you're doing, stop it!"

"Stop what? That's her own doing. I just whispered a little something in her ear. She likes tricks doesn't she? Magic tricks? I guess my magic trick is a little too much for her." He replied, callously looking away from her.

BORDEN WATCHED on as Olivia began to seize on the floor. The doctors clueless on how to assist her.

"Let her go!"

"Oh you're no fun."

"Olivia!" Borden shouted.

"You're wasting your breath. She can't hear you, no one here can hear you. Except that old bat probably. She's on my schedule soon. You should know that, right. I know you spoke to her at the docks. I don't know how you got in there, kind've ruined the surprise, but don't worry. You'll go back there soon enough."

Borden ignored Eidolon's taunts, shouting down at his wife.

"Olivia snap out of it!" Borden shouted once more.

"Did you not hear me? They can't hear you. You're an astral projection of yourself," Eidolon said, sighing out his disappointment. "Only those dead or soon to be, can see you. Which, by the way, you should be fully dead soon, or I'm going to be the least of your problems."

Eidolon pointed over at the other room, Patient Room D.

"Not gonna happen. Let her go."

"Fine, if you say so."

Borden watched as Olivia came to her senses. The doctors were all confused and traded looks with each other about her condition.

"There, you happy?"

"I'm gonna find my way out of here." Borden said.

"Well, maybe. It really depends on her now. Your body is too weak. The only thing keeping you alive is on this floor," Eidolon said, pointing at Olivia. "You're making a big mistake though. Your time in-between is running out and you're still latched."

He reached behind his back and revealed a paper boat.

Borden didn't know what the make of this.

"What is that?"

"A token, from yours truly," Eidolon said, pointing at Borden.

It placed the boat on Daisy's bedside table. "I hope she's

curious enough to unfold this. It has a lot of information that might just save her husband. After all, you wrote it to her." it said, laughing ominously.

"She's not going to fall for that." Borden replied.

"I guess we'll find out. Quite frankly, I'm a bit disappointed that it had to come down to this. It's for your own good."

THE EIDOLON's grasp tightened around Borden's neck in a split second.

"Time to go." He said, crushing Borden's windpipe.

The two of them vanished into thin air, leaving this timeline behind.

THUD!

Borden was spat out onto his office floor. Eidolon joined him soon after. They returned from their travels. Back to the fabricated house in Borden's fabricated reality.

"What the hell did you give her? What did you write?" Borden demanded.

"The truth, I suppose, just a little bent."

"Lies! You wrote lies! I didn't write that." He replied.

"Tricks, simple tricks. I simply need her to release you. My boss grows impatient and it's not that much amusement for me anymore. No offense," Eidolon replied. "Given that I can't take you in this condition, I'm just trying to speed up the process."

"I'm getting out of this place. She's not going to believe anything you tell her."

"I believe you, that's why **YOU** wrote the letter." He said, laughing with jubilation.

. . .

BORDEN SUDDENLY FELT NAUSEATED as he stumbled toward the floor. His insides decorated the carpet.

"What's happening?"

"Ah, see, it's funny how time works right? I simply planted a seed in that little escapade of ours. Coming back here and you'd be surprised to find the shade of a beautiful giant tree. She could have read that letter days, months, or even years ago."

Eidolon continued to speak as Borden struggled to stay conscious. "You see, Borden, time is just a construct. And in the realm beyond, it's even more malleable. I've been playing with time, and now it's catching up with you."

Eidolon's voice grew fainter as Borden's vision blurred. Borden tried to fight back, to resist the pull of his influence.

"No, I won't let you do this to me," he gasped, his body convulsing with pain.

But it was too late. Eidolon had already taken hold of him, and Borden knew he was lost. The last thing he heard before everything went black was the mocking laughter echoing in his ears.

IN THE WORLD of the living, Olivia was just about ready for bed. The house was still lonely and Borden's absence was palpable. She turned on her nightstand lamp and sat on the edge of her bed. The wind let a cool breeze into the room, enough to chill the air, but not freeze. She held the letter in her hand. Reading over it again and again. It was the only thing she had from Borden. The only thing that felt he was still there.

Is this really what you want me to do? You think this would really help you get out of there? I don't know if I have the strength to do it. But if you really think that it's the best chance we've got, then I trust you.

Her eyes traced the message once more, closely analyzing every letter, every word. It read:

Olivia, I hope this reaches you,

First and foremost I want to tell you that I love you. I always will. No matter what.

What I'm about to tell you is going to be very hard to believe, but I hope you can trust me when I say that it will all make sense in the end.

I'm at a place called the docks. I've been living with a fake version of you for what felt like years, but strange things started to occur. There's someone trying to keep me here. Permanently. To take me to the afterlife. Daisy is here. I saw her. She was at the docks.

Listen. This is going to sound extreme.

Your hold on me in the real world, limits my strength in this world. It's making it difficult to fight back. To escape. I need you to cut me off. I know I'm in a coma. You have to remove me from the life support. If you do that, I'll get stronger here and fight back the boatman. Trust me. Once I do that, I can find my way back to the world of the living. And be with you again.

Love always,

Borden.

Olivia’s tears fell onto the letter. She understood what he was asking for but it sounded counterproductive.

IT WAS ALREADY TOO LATE. Olivia's thoughts had already begun to take effect, and Borden was weakened as a result. Eidolon was now reaping what he had sowed, leaving Borden powerless and slipping towards the realm of the dying for good. And as fate would have it, the day of the special trip had arrived.

“It’s time Borden, time for the docks!”

16

CERTAINTY IN THE UNCERTAIN

There it is again. That awful sound. I remember that whistle.

Today's task was an extraordinarily daunting one for Olivia. As she got ready for work, she experienced a series of panic attacks, her heart racing and her hands shaking. Just thinking about what she was expected to do induced waves of nausea that threatened to overwhelm her. Despite having no appetite, she managed to force down a piece of toast, the dry bread sticking to the roof of her mouth.

As she made her way out of the house, her face wore a blank expression, but her mind was a flurry of thoughts and emotions. She could feel the cold metal of her keys in her pocket, the weight of her bag on her shoulder, and the scratchy fabric of her jacket against her skin.

Although she trusted Borden's instructions, something still felt wrong about it all. She could feel a knot of tension forming in her stomach, a sensation that wouldn't go away no matter how much she tried to distract herself. In an attempt to quiet the voices in her head, she turned to the car radio and was met with the song from the house.

"All Along the Watchtower?" she questioned, staring at her radio as she drove. The music enveloped her, the sound of the guitar strings vibrating in her chest.

"Borden, is this you?" she whispered, her voice barely audible over the music.

WALKING into the hospital felt like a journey of ten thousand steps for her. The doors felt so far away. People around her spoke, but no words came out of their mouths. Olivia was truly in her own head. Focused. Worried. Nervous. But determined. Determined to not let down her husband, who was counting on her. Olivia was nodding at her coworkers as she walked past, their replies muffled as if she were underwater. Olivia headed straight for the locker room to get ready.

As she entered the locker room, Olivia gasped for air, feeling as though a weight had been lifted from her chest. Her bag slipped off her shoulder, and she leaned heavily against a locker for support. A concerned coworker noticed her distress and came over to check on her.

"Olivia, are you okay? She asked.

Olivia looked up and noticed Sarah was coming out of the breakroom, which was just past the lockers.

"Sarah, hi, yes. I'm fine. I just have a big decision today to make," Olivia replied.

"What decision? You're sweating! Please, sit down. Talk to me."

Olivia took Sarah's arm for support as she guided her towards the center bench between the lockers.

"What decision are you making?" Sarah asked once more.

"Borden," Olivia replied, crying as she heard herself speak his name. "I think it's time I let him go."

OLIVIA DIDN'T WANT to go into the details of the letter because it sounded absurd. The last thing Olivia needed was to be committed to a psyche ward for her outlandish claims.

"Let him go? Olivia, that's a big deal. Why so sudden?"

"He's not getting any better, Sarah. I feel like he's only suffering in his condition."

Sarah looked at her, struggling to find a response to something that also had some validity to it. It was a sensitive issue. Sarah didn't want to make it seem as if she so easily accepted her decision as being the right thing to do, but part of her agreed with Olivia.

"Olivia, we just lost Daisy. I don't think, well. I just don't think this would be the best idea for you right now," Sarah suggested.

"That's the thing. It's not about what is best for me. It's what's best for Borden!"

"I hear you. I hear you."

. . .

Olivia's biggest fear as a doctor was always losing her patients. Her first experience with a lost patient had traumatized her for quite a while before she was able to rebound from it. Since then, she's been a little easier on herself, but that wasn't enough for the situation she was faced with today.

She was intentionally putting herself not only in that position but for Borden's sake. She'd be intentionally ending her husband's life based on the fact that a letter she had mysteriously received included instructions from Borden himself, that this would be the only way. It was only reasonable to expect Olivia to find this task to be the most difficult she would ever have to face. Willingly let her patient die.

"I don't know. I don't think it's fair to him that I keep holding on to him here. Maybe if he could speak, he would ask me to let him go."

"I know it's entirely up to you, and we'll support you in whatever decision you make. I just worry about you, ya know. I know what he means to you," Sarah said.

"Thanks, I appreciate that. I truly do. I think it might be for the best."

"In that case, I'm sorry, Olivia. I wish it worked out. I see your mind is made up. I admire your strength." Sarah replied.

"I'll see you in a bit. I'm just gonna get ready here."

Sarah nodded and rested her hand on Olivia's shoulder. After they traded solemn smiles, Sarah walked out of the locker room.

. . .

THE MINUTE THE DOOR CLOSED, Olivia broke down in hysterical tears. It was the first time she heard herself mention what she was planning to do out loud. She hated saying it; she hated thinking about it. She can't stand the idea of doing it. But there's no other way. That's what Borden said in the letter.

I truly hope I'm doing the right thing, Borden! It just sounds so crazy. You can't blame me for finding it difficult to do. This isn't easy. What if you're wrong, though? What if you can't do it? If that's the case, that disgusting filth won. It got what it wanted. I hate you for putting this on me. I hate you for asking me to do this.

Olivia grabbed the Polaroid from her locker and held it close to her chest.

"Borden, this better work, or I'll find a way to reach you and kill you myself. I love you."

"OLIVIA, I love you, but whatever it is you're doing, it's killing me!" Borden shouted as he continued to vomit on his office floor.

Across dimensions, Borden remained in a poor and weakened state. Eidolon's plan was working. It managed to trick Olivia into releasing Borden from his tether to the world of the living.

"It's no use, Borden, it's started. Look at you. It's over," Eidolon remarked, a sinister joy on his face.

"Olivia, please."

"She can't hear you. Don't you understand how pointless this is? Spare yourself some dignity and just come with me. Why prolong this any further? Don't you have an ounce of self-respect?"

"Shut up. Stop talking. I don't care what you did, nor what Olivia is doing. I know she'll do the right thing. I trust her." Borden said, struggling to his feet. "I'll find her, myself."

BORDEN USED the wall for assistance, reaching the frame of the mirror. He stood face to face with his reflection.

"What are you going to do? Travel? Go ahead," Eidolon said with a mocking gesture toward the mirror.

"I can do this."

"You can do this," Eidolon said, jokingly.

Borden looked back at him, dismissing his taunts.

"I CAN DO THIS."

"You're too weak. You can't travel in those conditions. That's not gonna work this time. Please, this is embarrassing."

"Come on! Turn on. I'm focused. Why aren't you fucking working?" Borden yelled, pounding the mirror repeatedly.

It was no use. The mirror continued its own form of mockery by reflecting the image of Borden's desperation.

"YOU WANT TO SEE OLIVIA? Do you?" Eidolon asked, gliding his way behind Borden. It placed one arm over his shoulder, and the other against the mirror.

Borden stood speechless as the mirror began to glow. The ripples began to radiate, and the flickering lights of the office gave a visual warning that something was starting to happen.

Powerful winds overtook the office decor, violently swirling around the two of them. Borden's hair was blowing back from the pressure of the mirror's magic unfolding before him. It was difficult for him to keep his eyes open.

"Look! There!" Eidolon shouted.

The mirror began to settle, forming a visual out of the water as the monstrous waves became calm. It was the hospital.

Eidolon had turned the mirror into a window. A window into Borden's room. Patient Room D. The room in which Borden's physical body existed.

"That's me," Borden muttered.

"Yeah, that is. Very perceptive."

"I don't get it."

"Keep watching."

The image soon became evident as some type of live-feed connection from his dimension into the real world. Olivia's body shortly entered the frame. She walked over to be at his side.

"Olivia," Borden said, whispering her name in bewilderment. "What trick is this?" he asked.

"Not a trick. You wanted to see her, well, here she is," Eidolon replied.

Normally, Eidolon's trickery and mischievous nature was expected, but there was a strange sincerity to what he was doing now.

"Olivia," Borden said, as his hand was lifted onto the mirror, placed over the image of his wife. "What is she doing?"

"I think we both know the answer to that question. Seems like it'll be time soon."

"Olivia! No! Please, Olivia!"

Borden began to gather the last bits of strength he had to shout at the mirror in hopes that she'd hear him, along with the pounding of his fist against the glass.

"Borden, listen. I know we've had our differences, but I hope you know this wasn't personal," Eidolon said, watching Borden's last attempt for a chance to live. "You have to understand that once you're on the list, you have to go. There's no way around it."

Borden with tears streaming down his face, his vocal cords straining with every shout, continued to barrage the mirror with his fist. "Olivia! Olivia!" He shouted repeatedly.

Olivia, in the mirror, was seen sitting next to Borden's body as if she were saying her final words to him.

Thud! Thud! Thud!

"Borden, please, I hope this is the best possible option we have. I,"—Olivia said, crying before she could finish her sentence.

Thud! Thud! Thud!

"What is that noise?" Olivia asked, looking over towards the window. It was faint, but she heard a knock. She turned back towards Borden's body. "Borden, was that you?"

"OLIVIA! OLIVIA! PLEASE, LOOK OVER HERE!" Borden screamed, pounding his fist.

Eidolon noticed with curiosity that Olivia did look toward them. "It's not gonna work, Borden."

Borden's knocks became weaker with each consecutive strike. His arm was getting tired. "Olivia! Please! Olivia!"

THUD! Thud!

Olivia looked once more toward the window, unknowingly staring at Borden, who watched in anguish as his wife was about to let him die.

"YES! That's it! Look over here. I'm here Olivia! Please wait! Don't do it!" Borden cried, his palms sliding down from the mirror, mustering all of his strengths to try to grab her attention.

But Olivia looked away.

"NO, NO, NO! OLIVIA! OLIVIA!" Borden yelled, one last time. It was no use.

"Olivia," he whispered in a broken cry, as he watched her return her attention to the body on the bed. Olivia began to disconnect Borden's breathing tube.

Eidolon's curiosity was soon washed away. It didn't work, as expected.

"There Borden, you saw her. I gave you that. Consider it a favor. We have to go."

Borden cried as he watched Olivia get up from the bed and began to walk away.

"Olivia...," he whispered.

Olivia approached the window in the room as if she were investigating the knocks she heard moments ago.

Borden looked up at the mirror and saw Olivia face to face with him. She was so close, and yet so far. His trembling hand managed to caress the glass, feeling as if he were sliding his hand down her cheek.

AT THAT MOMENT, Olivia, staring blankly at the window, reached up to her cheek with her own hand, "Borden?" she whispered.

"OKAY, TIME TO GO," Eidolon so callously interrupted what could've been a monumental and sentimental moment.

"No wait! Please!" Borden shouted.

The winds in the room settled down and the image of Olivia was broken and swept away as the mirror's particles reorganized themselves to shape into their original format. Borden returned to his own reflection.

"She saw me! I know it!" Borden cried.

"Listen, buddy. I know we're not the best of friends, but that's it. Time to go."

THE EARTH BEGAN TO RUMBLE, causing Borden to grip the edge of his desk tightly, his heart pounding in his chest. Suddenly, waves crashed through the windows of the office, sending papers flying and shattering glass everywhere. The sound was deafening, like the roar of a beast coming to devour them.

As the roof was ripped off, the exposed skies were unholy, like something out of a nightmare. The office began to flood, water pouring in at an alarming rate. Wooden planks began rising from the floor, creating a haphazard deck beneath his feet. The ship was coming to life, but it was not a comforting sight. Instead, it was a terrifying one. Borden's breaths came in short gasps as he realized the true scale of the disaster unfolding around him.

Sails were created out of the stacks of paper that existed on his desk and shelves, massive sails that flapped wildly in the storm. Borden clung to the floor not by choice but because his body could no longer function the way he wanted it to. The walls caved in themselves, exposing a vast ocean around them. The ocean was crimson as ever, like a sea of blood.

"Isn't she beautiful, Borden?" Eidolon asked, standing proud and tall by the rails of the ship.

BORDEN WAS SPEECHLESS AND WEAK. His vision was blurry, and he couldn't manage to keep his eyes open any longer.

"Hope you're not seasick. Long way to the docks!" Eidolon remarked, laughing with an insidious cackle.

Olivia, he thought to himself. *Olivia, I know you heard me. I know you felt me. Please, don't do it.*

Eidolon watched as Borden's consciousness faded away. "Well, that's no fun. He's gonna miss the sights," he said, grinning from cheek to cheek.

Eidolon began to whistle his ominous tune. The tune

was so recognizable and eery that it somehow managed to reach Olivia's thoughts.

That whistle.

Olivia stood in Borden's room. She turned back towards him. *There it is again. That awful sound. I remember that whistle.*

She stared at Borden as the machines spoke for him with a ceaseless beep.

I don't know about this Borden. I don't know.

Olivia began turning off the alarms and alerted her team.

"CODE STATUS: DNR - Do not resuscitate."

"Good-bye, Borden."

17

THE BEGINNING OF THE END

"That's fair, okay, be safe. Love you."

"Love you too."

A headset-wearing Borden settled comfortably in his office chair and folded a paper crane as he spoke with customers over the phone. The sun seeping through the blinds of his window provided sunlight to the potted plant on his desk. The aroma of vanilla-flavored coffee and paper filled the air.

Surrounded by paper, he was used to passing the time with his paper-folding art.

Borden noticed Olivia pass through the hallway as his chair swiveled toward the doorway. Holding the mic muffled with his hand, he called, "Olivia! Come here," before returning to his customer, "It's the best printer on the market, I can tell you that!"

Olivia stopped in the doorway.

Borden looked at her, gesturing with his free hand that he was hungry by patting his stomach.

Olivia pretended to not understand what he was trying to convey.

"Food, order food," he said under his breath, but the customer heard Borden, and he added, "Paper, order paper too. Can't have a printer without paper, right?"

Olivia laughed at his interaction and Borden pointed at her as if he was going to get her back for that.

"Hello?"

"Hello?"

"He hung up," Borden said.

Borden jumped out of his chair and chased Olivia out of his office.

"See what you made me do? Lost a client. Now you have to buy a printer."

"Oh, do I?" Olivia asked, a smile on her face.

"Yes, unfortunately, yes. Also a lifetime supply of paper. I take check or cash."

"Oh and how much would that be?"

"3.3 million dollars. Sorry, I don't make the rules." He said.

"Maybe you can sell all of those cranes you're making."

"Those? No. Those are priceless. Besides, a few hundred more and I get a wish granted." He said.

"What would you wish for?"

"A wife that orders me pizza when I'm hungry." He said, holding his stomach in hunger.

"You have to pick it up though." She said.

Borden walked back toward his office.

"Sounds good!"

Borden put on his shoes and grabbed his keys to head out.

"You're leaving already?" Olivia asked.

"Yeah."

"Borden, I just made the call. The pizza isn't ready yet."

"That's okay, I have an errand to run. Shouldn't take more than 5 minutes, I figure the pizza will be ready to pick up afterward." He said.

"That's fair, okay, be safe. Love you."

"Love you too."

Borden ignited the engine of his outdated car.

Still works.

He waved goodbye as Olivia watched him leave.

Borden turned on his radio and Jimi Hendrix was playing.

"Nice! Love this song." He said, jamming out to the guitar.

As the song crescendoed, without any moment to react, a speeding hunk of metal steamrolled straight into Borden's car, flipping violently down the street.

SPLASH!

Eidolon tossed a bucket of water at Borden's face.

"Wake up, Borden. You're missing the sights. Look at that scenery. Isn't it beautiful?"

Borden was too busy coughing out the water that traveled into his nose.

Eidolon was steering the ship not too far from where Borden was laying. The weakness in Borden's legs still plagued him. His dizziness and nausea as well.

"Are we there yet?" He asked.

"No of course not. You'll know when you see it, trust me."

"Trust you? You ruined my life."

"Don't blame me, I'm just the messenger, dear boy."

"You lied to Olivia."

"Yeah, I guess you're right." Eidolon replied, steering the ship. "It's for your own good."

"My own good is going back to my body and being with Olivia!"

"Don't be foolish. Your time is up. You have to understand that this is the best course of action for you." The Eidolon said.

"Fuck off."

THE WORLD around them reconfigured itself for a split second. It seemed to glitch like a flickering light.

"What was that?" Borden asked.

No response.

"Hey, what was that?"

"Shut up!" Eidolon called out, staring out in confusion, shaken up about the sudden glitch.

What was that? Was that you Olivia? What have you done?

INSIDE THE BORDEN RESIDENCE, a cloud of depression antagonized Olivia.

What do I do now? Do I just wait?

Haunted by her decision, granted it was Borden's apparent instruction, she couldn't help but feel as if she made a huge mistake.

The waiting just made everything worse.

Sitting on the edge of Borden's side of the bed, she read the note over and over again, wondering if she had missed anything.

"Is there something else?" She asked.

The letter was the only connection she had to Borden at this moment. By now, she had read it over a hundred times. Each time, hoping to find a clue she missed.

AND THEN IT HIT HER.

"THE CRANE!"

Olivia looked over at the nightstand, at the elegant wings of the crane that sat upon it.

The crane. Why did I never consider the crane? Surely, he wrote something in it too. If that boat had a secret message then the crane might have one also!

Her hands began the tedious process of unfolding such an intricate creation. She didn't want to tear it accidentally considering the sentimental value it held. Not just because of Borden's condition, but because it was the first crane she ever received from him.

Oh Borden, if you did something, this might just be the end of me as we know it.

She was getting closer to fully unwrapping this possible hidden message. Her trembling hands somehow managed to escape the fate of a dozen paper cuts.

Geez Borden, how many folds are there?

Finally, an exposed sheet of paper. There they were. The words of her husband. The tears that filled her eyes from sorrow turned to tears of joy.

You're magic. You're absolute magic!

Olivia read the note.

if there's something special you want to

wish for, Add this crane to a pile of 999 or more.

-Angier Borden

"Borden, you can't be serious." She said, gathering her composure. "This is the secret? A wish? Do you think I'm going to make 1,000 cranes and hope for a wish? Borden, this can't be the only option? I took you off life support. Like you told me. Just to hope for a wish?"

Olivia was a bit distressed, holding both letters up against each other as if she were arguing with Borden in real-time.

Wait a minute.

Olivia inspected the note for a closer look.

"Angier Borden," she said, puzzled.

She lifted the other note into closer proximity to her eyes.

"Borden," she said.

That's strange, two different letters, with two different sign-offs. Borden always signs off with his full name, why is this letter missing it?

THAT'S when the reality hit her like a ton of bricks.

That wasn't a secret letter from her lover.

That wasn't the plan of her husband, Borden.

"The eidolon! This wasn't from Borden!" She shouted.

With tears streaming down her face, she began to spiral into a moment of guilt.

"What have I done? Borden! I thought that was from you! I need to go, maybe there is still time!"

She took a glance at the crane letter.

Wait. Maybe, that's the actual plan. Borden, I don't have time to—

"Your cranes!"

HER SCENT of desperation overtook the offices' dusty odor. Olivia ran inside on a mission. To find the cranes.

Okay Borden, where did you keep them? That mass amount of cranes you've folded over the years with your silly little wish plan.

Boxes upon boxes, being knocked over as Olivia rummaged throughout the entire office.

"Where is it?" She shouted.

THERE IT WAS. The box of cranes. Thousands of them.

Hold on Borden. Hold on.

18

THE ESCAPE ARTIST

You fool! There's no use for doing this? Do you not understand?

The world around Borden and Eidolon's journey continued to glitch. An occasional tear in the fabric of their reality every so often occurred. Eidolon appeared confused at the sight of it. Something he hadn't seen before, or at least not in a long time.

But he carried on steering the ship.

Borden was sitting up against the rail of the ship, staring up at the skies that couldn't decide on what wall-paper to settle for. Borden felt as though someone was messing around with the desktop screensaver.

He was distracted anyway. Suddenly, a surge of power rushed through him. His legs stiffened. His arms were no longer noodles.

He didn't want to draw any attention from Eidolon.

It's best he thinks that I'm still weak as before. I don't know why this is happening, but I'm not complaining.

He looked down before him, a puddle. A small, but big enough puddle for Borden to see his reflection in.

This is it. My ticket out of here.

"Hi, are you Olivia Borden?"

"Yes, I am. Who is this?"

The awful cries of a woman in complete hysterics hauntingly rang inside the heads of the gathered crowd. Olivia stepped out of her car screaming in disbelief. Neighbors and passersby made their way as she walked between them. A police officer maintaining the peace stopped in her tracks.

"We can't have anyone cross here."

"That's my husband!" Olivia cried.

She ran onto the scene. The paramedics were already there. The aftermath of a terrifying car crash left Borden's car unrecognizable and flipped upside down on a neighbor's lawn.

"Borden!"

"Borden!"

"Ma'am, I'm sorry, but we need to get him to a hospital."

"Is he alright? I'm a doctor. Please, let me help!"

"He's already loaded, we're headed there now."

"Yes, okay! I'll ride with you. I work at that hospital. Please, tell me. Is he alright?"

"He's breathing. Not conscious, but breathing. Let's go."

"Borden..."

Olivia opened her eyes and stared at the crane in front of her. Reliving that awful day, she cried as she made a wish. It took her a while before she was able to make the letter back into a crane, but she did it.

She took the box of cranes she found and immediately dumped them onto the office floor. There were thousands of them. Thousands. So many paper cranes.

Okay Borden, here goes.

Olivia brought the paper crane up to her lips. Pursed, they made contact with the paper and ink that had existed for over 10 years.

My wish Borden.

My wish for you is that you come back to me. Make it back and stay with me. Please. Come back.

She lowered the paper crane carefully onto the pile. The crane that started it all. It sat on that little paper crane hill. Defeated and roughed up from the years of living in the nightstand drawer.

She stared with eager anticipation. Waiting for something to occur.

Is there something I need to do? A specific saying? Borden, I don't know. Nothing's happening.

KNOCK KNOCK!

Someone was at the door.

"Borden is that you?" She asked.

She ran out of the office, tears in her eyes, shouting, "Borden! You're back, you did it!"

Her hand gripped the doorknob with built-up passion and anxiety.

She swung the door open.

"Borden?"

No one was there.

Borden stared at the puddle, mustering all of his strengths into one last attempt to escape. Eidolon looked at Borden, curious about the sudden silence.

"No! Where are you going?"

Borden had plunged himself through the puddle, his feet being the last thing Eidolon saw. Immediately, Eidolon leaped down and managed to follow Borden before the puddle reconfigured itself back to normal.

A hand latched onto Borden's shoulder as he fell through the lights of time. The destination was up ahead, and they both collapsed into it.

"Where are we?"

"You fool! There's no use for doing this? Do you not understand?" Eidolon asked, growing annoyingly impatient.

"This is, my house?" Borden asked, knowing that it indeed was his house.

His return was so close, and yet still so far, no matter how much closer he got.

"Borden. You need to come with me." Eidolon said.

Borden scrambled to his feet and ran up the driveway toward the door.

"Borden!"

"Shut up!"

Borden's fist pounded on the door.

"Come on Olivia! Open the door!" He shouted.

Eidolon grabbed Borden's shirt and conjured a portal, yanking him through it.

"We're leaving!"

They were gone. The door opened and Olivia stepped out.

OLIVIA STARED at the vast nothingness outside of her door. Expecting Borden to be standing there with open arms for her to fall into. Imagining herself finally out of this massive nightmare. But he wasn't.

It didn't work. I need to go to the hospital. I have to do something!

Olivia ran back inside the house with the stench of defeat around her. She felt like an idiot, believing a letter that said to unplug her husband from life support as being the best possible option.

How stupid.

Walking into the office for her car keys, she noticed something strange. The cranes. The thousands of paper cranes that were piled on the floor.

They were gone.

Olivia was stunned at the sight, her hands concealing the words she couldn't speak.

"Borden! The cranes! They're gone! Borden, it worked!" She shouted, crying with tears of joy and amazement. "Borden, I'll see you soon!"

Like a person on the brink of insanity, she ran out of the house shouting for Borden. Turned on the car, and steadfast toward the hospital. Speeding down the highway, she looked at the Polaroid of Borden, smiling at the thought of him.

RING! RING!

"Hello?"

"Olivia, hi! You need to come to the hospital, quick."

"I'm on my way!"

"It's Borden. He's, well, I think you should just see for yourself."

"Thanks, Sarah!"

19

EVERYTHING THAT WILL HAPPEN, HAS ALREADY HAPPENED

You can't stay here. You have to trust me on this one.

The surrounding lights and images that engulfed Borden and Eidolon as they fell through the portal flashed as they pushed and tugged each other.

"Let me go!"

"You can't escape this," Eidolon replied.

Falling and scrapping with each other, they emerged into one of the images, appearing inside a car together.

"Where are we now?"

"I'm trying to tell you. Nothing matters. Your fate is sealed." Eidolon responded, steering the car.

Borden in the passenger seat, gazed out of the window to try and orient himself with the destination they entered. It looked familiar, but he couldn't pinpoint the location.

An idea came across Borden, as he brought down the windshield sunshade, exposing the vanity mirror. It was a long shot, but he was willing to try.

"What are you doing?" Eidolon asked, noticing as Borden fidgeted. "Stop that, I know what you're trying to do it won't work."

"I don't care what you think." Borden replied, focusing on the vanity mirror."

To Eidolon's surprise, the mirror as small as it was, began reconfiguring itself into a portal. He attempted to stop Borden from leaving.

"No, stop that, you can't!" Eidolon shouted, one hand at the wheel and the other at the sunshade.

"Stop!" Borden shouted. "Let me go!"

The car began to swerve.

They were approaching an intersection.

Traveling at a remotely fast speed, Eidolon was too busy trying to stop Borden from leaving through the vanity mirror, he didn't notice the person crossing the street.

"Look out!" Borden shouted, taking the wheel into his own hands and shifting away from the pedestrian.

The car shifted away and nearly missed the crossing child, but plowed straight into a car.

The victim's car rolled countless times before landing in a neighbor's yard.

Dazed and confused, Borden came to his senses, realizing what had just happened.

"Holy shit!"

Eidolon was quite rattled himself, but quickly shook off the accident. Borden ran outside of the car, making his way through thick smoke and metal debris scattered all over the asphalt.

"Please be okay, please be okay." He muttered to himself as he approached the car.

The car was beyond recognizable.

The person behind the wheel was not.

It can't be.

Eidolon walked to Borden's side. There was a sense of sympathy in his steps. A sympathy toward Borden.

"Now do you see?" He asked.

"It doesn't make sense," Borden said.

Borden approached the car for a closer look inside the cabin. Sitting in the driver's seat, was himself. Borden.

"The accident? This is what put me in a coma? This is what put me in this shit show? Did I put myself here? I did this?"

Eidolon was silent.

Borden turned to Eidolon, tears in his eyes, "How is this possible? Tell me!"

Eidolon didn't utter a word.

Borden's attention was brought toward the child on the sidewalk. The child he saved by swerving the car out of her direction.

"That girl," Eidolon said."You saved her Borden."

"I saved her?" Borden asked.

"You made a choice, and albeit a noble one, it cost you dearly," Eidolon replied.

"But you put me in this position! You were driving the car."

"When will you realize, I'm nothing more but a collector. A transporter. A messenger. I pick up the souls of those that are already gone. Nothing you try or do, will change that fact."

. . .

A CROWD BEGAN to form at the scene, including neighbors, and patrol cars. A policeman arrived and began to maintain the scene of the incident, preventing curious eyes from wandering too close.

"We need to go," Eidolon said.

"I'm not going anywhere."

"You don't want to be here, trust me."

"Why not?"—

A CAR PULLED up to the scene, a familiar car.

"Olivia?"

"We need to go now, Borden."

Borden inched closer, but still viewing from afar. His eyes began to overflow with tears.

"Olivia, I'm sorry." He cried. "I'll make my way back to you."

Borden's spirit broke at the sight of his wife experiencing such tragedy.

Eidolon's hand rested on Borden's shoulder, a sympathetic touch.

"We're leaving."

A portal opened behind them, and Borden took a step backward, not looking away from his wife. A flash of brightness overtook him. He was falling once again through the lights of time.

Traveling through the portal, Borden didn't seem to put up much of a fight. He was willingly returning wherever Eidolon was sending them.

Finally, they land, emerging once more on the ship that was taking Borden across to the realm of the dead. Eidolon was exhausted. The time dilation was very taxing to be repeating as often as he had. All of that traveling took a toll on the spiritual and physical well-being of the traveler.

Borden, himself, too was tired. He wasn't very expressive. His face was blank. Reflective. Eidolon noticed this and extended an attempt to console the man.

"Borden."

"I don't want to hear it." He replied.

Borden, a man who had realized that all of his decisions were meant to lead to this point. His varied attempts, time traveling, dimension-hopping, everything was futile. There was no more use in trying.

"Borden," Eidolon continued. "Everything that will happen, has already happened."

Borden looked up at him.

"What about Olivia? She was helping me get out of this until you fucked it up!"

"Olivia is prolonging the inevitable. If anything, it could only make matters worse."

"What do you mean?"

"Those that cannot accept their fate, are torn in two at the docks. Something much worse lies ahead for those that cannot let go of what is already gone."

THE WORLD around the ship began to glitch again. Eidolon didn't take this very lightly.

"Borden, listen to me very carefully." He said, gazing at the skies around them.

Borden too, was hypnotized by the skies reconfigurations. A storm broke out and powerful winds began to conjure waves that crashed onto the ship.

"What's happening?" Borden shouted.

A waterfall emerged ahead of them. Not a normal one. Borden's eyes almost shot out of his head as he witnessed the behemoth trail of water that ascended into the sky.

"Is that a waterfall? Going up?" Borden shouted, questioning if he was seeing the right thing.

"Yeah, it is," Eidolon responded.

"We're headed right for it. Do something!"

"I can't, the boat is moving on its own now. It's being sucked into that thing."

"What do we do?"

Borden and Eidolon continue to shout at each other, having difficulty speaking due to the vicious winds and thunderous roars of the skies breaking apart. The ship's planks began tearing away.

"What do we do?"

Eidolon looked at Borden for a moment, astonished at what he saw.

"Borden? You? You're still latched? How is this possible?"

"What do you mean?"

You're not ready, you can't be here. That waterfall, you can't go into it!"

"Where does that lead?"

"Limbo."

"What does that mean."

"A fate much worse than death."

Eidolon seemed to struggle, as he became visibly in pain. He was still in a weakened state from the traveling.

"I can't exist this close to that realm, I'm going to fade soon."

"Get us out of here!"

"I can't, I'm too weak now. You find a way. You must."

—

. . .

A ROARING WAVE crashed onto Eidolon's body and swept him away in the process.

"Hey! Where'd you go?" Borden shouted, alone on the ship headed to its imminent doom.

Borden ran to look over the rails of the ship. The crimson waters were a terrifying sight, but he figured he had no other options.

"I have to jump," he said with a lack of confidence.

Looking back to the gravity-defying waterfall, beckoning his gaze, something came over him.

"What if I'm being tricked again?" Borden asked himself.

The monstrous waterfall inching closer to sweep him away.

"This is all a ploy! Olivia figured something out and that's my ticket out. He's trying to trick us again. Of course!"

His attention returned back down to the water below as he contemplated abandoning the ship. Turning toward the floor, he stared at his reflection in the water that had accumulated over the planks.

"Come on. Open"

No result. His desperate reflection rippled back to him.

"Please, open."

Nothing happened.

Waves crashed over his body, the ship beginning to collapse as it got closer to the waterfall.

"Fuck!"

He ran back to the railing.

Looked down at the height of the jump.

"That's a really big fucking jump."

Closed his eyes and spoke to Olivia with his thoughts.

Olivia, I'm so sorry for what I've put you through. Don't worry about the letter or whatever it is you did. I know you tried your best to save me. I love you so very much—

Just then.

He opened his eyes, and something strange occurred.

A single paper crane.

A single paper crane was floating alongside him.

A crane?

20

IN A WHITE ROOM

“Olivia! I’m almost home!” He cried.

The sound of Olivia’s footsteps echoed through the hospital corridors as she hurried toward Patient Room D. Her heart was filled with anxiety and nervousness as she pushed through the doors. Inside, a team of doctors was huddled around Borden, deep in concentration.

“I’m here. What’s going on?” She asked.

The team of doctors turned simultaneously toward her and gave each other solemn stares before one of them said, “It’s his heart. It seems steady, and his breathing is regulated. We think he might wake up soon.”

Olivia’s knees buckled as she heard that, boosting her hope for Borden’s return.

“Please, Olivia, take a seat. Don’t work yourself up. You don’t want to end up here yourself.” A resident said.

"Borden, I knew you'd come back," Olivia said

Borden was still strapped to machines that spoke for him with a variety of beeps. Every passing sound only made Olivia's anxiety grow larger.

"I've never seen anything like this," one resident said to another.

"Yeah me neither." He replied.

Olivia's attention was completely fixated on Borden. As she stood next to him, she couldn't help but tune out the chatter of the surrounding doctors. It was as though they were in their own world, with their own private conversation. Her mind was racing with thoughts about Borden - his health, his well-being, and his future.

She was so engrossed in her own thoughts that she barely noticed when one of the doctors tried to speak to her. It wasn't until they called her name twice that she snapped back to reality. Embarrassed, she apologized and tried to refocus on the conversation at hand. But her mind kept drifting back to Borden.

Every little detail about him caught her attention. It was as though she was trying to absorb every aspect of him, to better understand him and his condition. She couldn't bear the thought of missing any clue or insight that could help him in his recovery.

The more she thought about Borden, the more she felt a sense of responsibility toward him. She was determined to be there for him every step of the way, to advocate for him, to ensure that he received the best care possible. Her focus on him was unwavering, and she knew that nothing could distract her from her goal of helping him.

"Wait a minute!" Olivia said.

Borden's heart rate began to skyrocket.

"What's happening?"

"I don't know. He was fine a second ago."

"We need to drop it fast!" Olivia shouted.

"Quick! antiarrhythmic drugs STAT!" a resident called out.

"Good, yes!"

Olivia watched in horror as Borden was battling against whatever was going on in his head. She was determined that he would get through it.

A CRANE?

That's a crane, a paper crane. Did I make that?

"Olivia! She opened the crane!" Borden shouted, climbing down from the railing of the ship. "This has to mean something."

The lonely paper crane was drifting alongside the ship, headed for the same fate as Borden. To be sucked up by the antigravity waterfall.

"It's headed that way, too. What do I do?" Borden wondered.

Borden's heart was pounding as he surveyed the chaotic scene around him. The once-sturdy ship was now barely holding together, the sails in tatters, flapping uselessly in the raging winds. The rain was pouring down in sheets, making it difficult to see anything beyond a few feet in front of him. He could hear the sound of wood splintering and cracking as the ship was battered by wave after wave.

Borden knew he had to act swiftly if he wanted to survive. He looked around desperately, searching for any sign of help or a way out. But there was nothing.

"Do I jump? Do I stay? What do I do?"

To Borden's amazement, several more cranes made an appearance, floating alongside the ship as well.

"There's more! They're all headed that way? Is this a sign? Am I supposed to go in there? Maybe Eidolon was trying to keep me from going up there? Maybe this is the way!" He shouted.

The ferocious breeze generated by the waterfall grew stronger, spraying his face with its mist. The sheer intensity of the wind was enough to blow away a large portion of the ship's structure, leaving him exposed to the elements.

"I have to decide now. There's no more time!"

He looked back down at the paper cranes, and his doubts were put to an end.

THOUSANDS OF PAPER cranes began flooding the waters next to him, all leading toward the waterfall!

"There's so many! It has to be. The wish. She made the wish! Oh, Olivia! I could kiss you right now! I love you! This has to be you!"

Borden felt the courage and bravery of all of those cranes combined. His mental fortitude became a steel trap, and doubt had left his body.

"This is you, Olivia. I stay. That has to be the way!"

The ship began to incline. Everything slowly slid down to the back of the ship, Borden included.

He gripped the railing that still looked sturdy enough to hold him and within seconds, his body was hanging vertically, parallel to the waterfall.

"Hold on! I have to hold on!"

The ship was ascending, but as it climbed higher, it began to break apart under the powerful currents. However, as Borden looked ahead, he saw a glimmer of light in the distance, like an exit at the end of a tunnel. It was the brightest light he had ever seen, yet it didn't hurt his eyes.

The ship's creaks and groans grew louder as it ascended higher. The weight of the vessel proved too great for the steep climb, causing the railing to detach from the main structure. With a crash, the ship collapsed back down, plummeting to its destruction. Borden's eyes were drawn below him, and he watched in horror as the vessel was consumed by the depths.

"Holy shit! I can't fall now."

One of his hands slipped from the railing, and he was now dangling what could've been over 500 feet in the air. The waterfall roared, and the gushing currents continued to pull him up.

The light was getting brighter and brighter, and the winds were heavier and heavier. The thunderous claps in the sky became the soundtrack of this final journey.

"I can see something. I'm almost there."

As he looked to his right and left, he saw that he was accompanied by thousands of paper cranes, each one a symbol of hope and perseverance that had made his journey possible. Together, they continued to climb upstream against the current of the enormous waterfall.

"Olivia! I'm almost home!" He cried.

He was finally consumed by the illumination, and the brightness overwhelmed his eyes. It was as though he had entered a vacuum, where everything had settled into a state of absolute stillness and silence.

Everything ceased all at once.

* * *

The bright light became tolerable, and the surroundings began to emerge into recognizable structures. The bright light, a fluorescent light bulb, hung over Borden's head.

Beep.

Beep.

Beep.

"Borden!" Olivia cried.

"Hello?"

"Borden! Oh my god, Borden! You're awake!"

The hospital room erupted into a symphony of cheers as everyone bore witness to Borden's miraculous recovery. Doctors hugged one another, shook hands, and, most importantly, looked over at Olivia's big cheesy smile. Tears overflowed not just from Olivia's eyes, but from those of her colleagues and everyone else present in the room.

"Borden!"

"Olivia, is that you?"

"Yes, it's me, you idiot! How could you put me through that? Oh my god, it worked!"

"What worked?" Borden asked, dazed from his condition.

"The wish! I made the wish Borden!"

"Wow, I can't believe it. So that's what did it, huh?" Borden asked.

Olivia was thrilled, jumping up and down, hugging Borden tightly, not wanting to let him go.

"What am I in for?"

"A head injury, for real this time," Olivia said, laughing at how everything had returned full circle.

"And what are you in for?"

"What?"

. . .

EVERYONE in the room besides Borden and Olivia began to melt down into the floor. The walls began to crumble.

"What's going on? Borden?"

"You just couldn't let him go, huh?" Borden asked.

"Borden?" she asked, fright in her shaking voice.

Olivia looked around frantically. "Where did everyone go?"

"This is what you wanted to see, isn't it? Borden coming back. Safe and sound. Beautiful fairy tale ending. This is how you live these days? Replaying this moment over and over. I had to come to see for myself."

"Borden, this isn't funny!" She cried.

"This isn't Borden! This is you, in your head! I'm just paying a little visit because Borden isn't on my list anymore, which could only mean one thing."

Olivia's body felt as if it were shutting down, all of her blood rushing, pooling to the bottom of the floor. She couldn't breathe, she couldn't process anything, she was completely immobile.

"I warned him. He didn't listen. The same way you didn't listen. I hope it was worth it. It's poetic, I suppose. Worlds apart once more, dimensions apart, both of you in some type of limbo. A true romantic tragedy. I'll see you around when it's your time."

"W-w-wait! No, this isn't real. Borden came back!" She screamed.

EIDOLON DISAPPEARED, and the hospital bed materialized into an empty white bed. The walls began to contort into cushioned walls. Paint began to overflow from the top to the bottom, a bright white. All four walls, without any windows.

"I saved him! No, this isn't real! I saved Borden! He came back! I saved him!" She screamed, her veins popping out from the frustration of her shouts.

A team of doctors barged into the room, grabbing her and strapping her down onto the bed.

"Dr. Borden, please! Calm down!"

"Sedate her, sedate her!" One of them shouted.

Olivia's screams continued, "I SAVED HIM! I SAVED HIM! THE CRANES! THE LETTER! THE GRAVEYARD! THE MONSTERS! IT WAS THE EIDOLON'S FAULT! THE BOATMAN!"

The men struggled but managed to sedate her.

"It was me. I saved him. Borden, you're here, I know it. I wished with the cranes." She said, her voice fading as the drugs kicked in. "I saved him...I unplugged his life support. I saved him. The letter. The boatman..."

"Borden..."

"Borden..."

"I saved you..."

Olivia's last words brought immense sadness to Mariana, as she watched from outside the door standing close to two psychiatric nurses. Her child, her little girl, is reduced to this. It broke her heart.

"Olivia," she said, her voice breaking as she witnessed her condition worsening.

"I'm sorry. It doesn't seem to be getting any better. It's been eight months, and she still wakes up to the same story."

"How much longer do you think she'll be here?" Mariana asked, struggling to form her words.

"We don't know. Every once in a while, during her

therapy sessions, she seems to understand, but then she begins to rant about the letters from a spirit that tricked her into unplugging Borden from his life support. Or a paper crane 'wish' that worked. She talks about visions she saw and things that spoke to her. Unfortunately, her delusions remain the same."

Mariana cried as she listened to her daughter's situation.

"Unfortunately, when Borden died that day, Olivia's psyche couldn't take it. She had a psychotic breakdown. It was too much. At this point, we believe she's suffering from schizophrenia. It's been long enough for her to still have symptoms of psychosis. As far as she knows, Borden came back." The nurse said. "It's pretty common for a traumatic event to trigger such a thing. We will do all we can to try to help, but she's pretty far gone. I'm sorry."

Mariana nodded and stared into the small door window. Her daughter was knocked out cold. She looked peaceful in her sleep. Mariana's mouth quivered.

"You mentioned letters?" She asked.

"Yes, apparently there were letters she got from a spirit and one from Borden. We looked into it. There were no letters. She mentioned the boatman, and we don't know a boatman. We talked to the receptionist, who claimed to have a conversation about a guy she saw in the locker room, but she said he didn't exist."

Mariana understood the situation. Though reluctant, she knew she had no other option. As she cast a final glance toward the window, she placed her palm on it and then brought her hand back to her heart.

"Goodbye, baby. I'll come by again next week. I hope you feel better. I know Angi wishes the same for you. I love you, Oli."

. . .

Olivia lay on a white bed, on white furniture, in a white room, without any windows aside from the door.

She had on a white gown.

Her eyes were open.

Her back faced the door window, so she appeared asleep.

But she was awake.

She was whispering to herself. A grin on her face. Joy.

"Borden, I'm so glad you're back Borden!"

"What will we do today?"

"Show me a magic trick, Borden! Please."

"I love your magic tricks."

"The wish worked, Borden!"

"I saved you."

"I saved you."

"I saved you."

Borden found himself standing ankle-deep in water, engulfed by an endless silence that echoed through a void of black nothingness. There was nothing around him, only an impenetrable darkness that was somehow illuminated enough for him to discern the shape of a crane.

The crane?

The single crane floated toward him, bumping into his ankle.

"Hello?...ello...llo...lo...o" He shouted, his voice echoing before fading.

"Olivia...livia...ivia...via...ia...a"

. . .

MORE CRANES BEGAN FLOATING around him.

"OLIVIA...LIVIA...IVIA...VIA...IA...A"

"ANYONE?...NYONE?.. YONE?...ONE?.. NE?...E?"

HE REMAINED MOTIONLESS, his countenance betraying the realization that his fate had been prophesied. His existence had been reduced to a state of perpetual confinement, with no prospect of escape.

With a soul-crushing, defeated voice, he uttered a final whisper, resigned to his interminable captivity.

"OLIVIA..."

THE END

Acknowledgments

I'd like to thank Zachary Riggs, for reading some early drafts of this story. Your feedback was appreciated.

To Brianne. Thank you for constantly letting me chew your ear off with my dailies. Your suggestions were validated and implemented throughout and I am grateful for that.

To the readers: I truly hope you enjoyed this little story. It was exciting to create and an experience I won't forget. I appreciate your support. Thank you.

ABOUT THE AUTHOR

My name is Miguel Sandoval. I am an artist / musician. I specialize in charcoal and pencil portraits. I have an affinity for the psycho-thriller genre of films. This novel was an experiment for myself, as well as a possible way to bring a movie script I had in mind, to life.

I wrote this for myself, but I hope anyone that reads it can find it enjoyable.

Feel free to reach out to me on social media to talk about the book, or life in general. Thanks.

instagram.com/miggstyv